A VERY FRACTURED JUL

PIECES OF THE PRISM

GRAF
MAY

An Elesara Series Novel
Published by 252 Publishing LLC
901 Brutscher Street, Ste. D252
Newberg, OR 97132

ISBN 978-1-950753-02-4 (print)
ISBN 978-1-950753-03-1 (eBook)
Library of Congress Control Number:2019921150

For Penny,
Find yourself and pick you up, and all your life you'll have good luck.

For Nathan,
A love for words is forged.

INTRODUCTION

The following fictitious events take place in the Blue Universe

1

DOUBT

It was a Jul of doubt.

They stood in the stable with a woven sack of carrots and grains and apples, giving treats to the horses.

Well, mostly Niels gave treats to the horses. Cille had decided to eat one of the apples, and Viggo gave most of his treats to the floor. "Pick them up!" Niels groaned. He tried to show Viggo: "You give them to the horses like *this*."

Viggo spread some of the grains on the floor and drew a picture in them.

It wasn't a bad picture. Niels turned away and let him keep drawing so he wouldn't get in the way again. Their parents had left them alone in the stable; it was the seed of his doubt. If Julemanden *really* came with his sleigh and his reindeer while all of them were at church, why did his parents go inside first? What were they *doing*, if not putting presents under the tree?

He passed the sack to Cille, in her fluffy red-and-white fur dress. "Your turn," he told her, and he ran out of the stable before she could tell him no. He ran through the cold and the dark. The snow was so light he could see grass, and with every step he took snow puffed around his feet, pushed aside by air.

He went in the back door, which led down to the cellar or up to the kitchen. He slipped in silently and let the door click shut behind him before he paused, there on the landing, ears primed to catch his parents in the act of pretending to be Julemanden.

They were not in the blue room where the Jul tree stood; they were in the kitchen, and Niels could smell cookies frying on the stove. Far sang, teasing Mor: "It's hard to be a Nissemand." It was a song for kids, about how elves had to work on Jul when everyone else got to stay home from school and play. It was in a mix of Danish and English, which Niels loved to learn any time Far spoke it.

Mor laughed. "You should be more careful," she scolded, but Far only sang louder.

Niels stepped into the doorway in time to see them: Far — dressed in the red furs and long white-trimmed cloak of Julemanden — swung Mor into a twirl that spun her partway around the kitchen and landed her in his arms, where he kissed her.

His eyes widened when he looked over her shoulder and saw Niels in the doorway. He stepped away from her. "Glædelig Jul!" He swung Niels in an arc and landed him right next to Mor, who of course had to kiss his head and tell him Glædelig Jul too.

"Far!" he greeted. He tried to shrug Mor off, but she wanted more hugs. "I thought you were Julemanden."

Now he had his proof; Far did the presents every year while they were in the stable.

But Far misunderstood: "A costume, to surprise you with," he said. It wasn't a confession at all.

Had...had Niels missed something? If Far didn't *know* he suspected, maybe there was nothing to suspect; maybe Julemanden was real.

Maybe *magic* was real.

Niels stepped further into the room. "Can I help cook?" If they let him help, that would be real magic at work.

Mor put on her *no* face. "Not this year, it isn't safe."

It would never be safe; it was the same refusal Niels heard every year. He was too little, it wasn't safe.

Far made pouty lips at Mor. "He's almost a man," he argued.

He was?

A thrill ran through him. *Almost a man*.

Mor made her *no* face even more, and Far sighed and looked at him. "Presents?" he suggested.

Yes, presents! He was *almost a man* enough to accept no; enough to think of his sister and brother too. "What about Cille and the baby?"

Far chuckled and laughed with Mor about how Viggo was almost old enough for school. "They will come," he promised Niels. "We will sing loud enough that they hear us and come inside."

Mor turned off the burner, and the sounds of oil pops slowed down. She grabbed a plate of already-cooked klejner and walked with them toward the blue room. "I'm not sure Julemanden brought you gifts this year," she warned Niels. "Cille told him you upset her."

Maybe magic *wasn't* real. Not because he believed he wouldn't get presents, but because Mor thought he was that gullible.

"Don't listen to her," Far whispered. "He would never forget you."

Mor bumped into Far. Niels bet they would kiss again, and he would have to watch, but all Far did was nuzzle her with his forehead. "You, on the other hand..." he teased. "Julemanden said you were naughty all year."

"Very," she laughed. And then *she* kissed Far and Niels ducked his head and ran into the blue room ahead of them so he wouldn't have to watch.

In the blue room, Far opened shutters on the window nearest the stable, and lifted the top of the window so it was open. He bellowed the Nissemand song out the window, so Cille and Viggo would hear. He looked at Niels, inviting — daring? — him to join in.

He sighed, and he sang too, and it was fun even though he was sure it wouldn't be. Jul was weird like that. Life was more fun, just because it was today. That was magic. Watching the snow scatter around Cille and Viggo as they ran inside with the mostly-full bag of carrots, apples, and oats. That was magic too, and so was the sound of them as they stomped up the stairs and rushed into the room.

"Mor!" Cille yelled. "Presents!" She hugged their mom and jumped onto her knees in front of the tree, hoarding presents toward herself. "All of these are mine," she announced. "The Nisse said boys are too bad to get presents."

"Mine!" Viggo yelled. "All mine!"

Niels was older now; almost a man. He sat on the couch near his parents and waited, like adults did.

"Søn," Far called to Viggo, "come out. Help me eat this treat."

Viggo stopped trampling the presents and looked out at them between the branches. "Treat?" He ran in again — or tried to, anyway, but Mor caught him and swung him up and into her arms. "Presents!" he yelled, trying to get away.

Mor passed him a gift and he settled on the couch, ready to tear into it like a wolf.

Mor passed Niels a gift too: "This is for you," she said.

It was long, almost as big as Niels even if it weighed a lot less, and wrapped in a gold and black paper that made him feel even older than the *almost a man* comment.

"It looks special," Mor commented.

It was heavy, almost too heavy for him to move easily. He looked at the tag: It said it was from Julemanden.

Carefully, he unwrapped it, to discover a box, and inside the very large box was...a guitar! A real, just for him, guitar!

He looked up at Far. "Will you teach me?"

Far loved music; he even played at family parties. Not just for the children, either; adults liked his performances. It wasn't like their cousin Eddie. *He* could play piano for auditoriums full of people who paid to be there. People called him vidunderbarn...prodigy.

Niels would never be that good, but he knew he would love the guitar.

He strummed it while Far unwrapped a gift from Mor. It was a set of guitar picks, hand painted. Niels grinned at Far; they could play together.

Then Far was gross again and kissed Mor for way too long, but when he stopped he held his hand out to Niels and passed him one of the guitar picks. "This one is for you," he said.

It was blue, the color of faded spray paint on a gray wall.

Niels played even louder with the pick, and watched while his brother and sister opened their presents.

Viggo tried to grab Niels' guitar. "I want one!"

Niels should have been mad, but he couldn't be. That was the magic of the Jul. He reached for a long present under the tree and handed it to Viggo. "Julemanden got you something too," he said. He watched the wonder in Viggo's eyes when he found what was under the paper and pressed the buttons on his electronic kid guitar.

Because it was Jul, he and Viggo did a concert for their parents. They played "It's Hard to Be a Nissemand," and their parents laughed and clapped.

In a few minutes, the rest of the presents were opened and the paper disposed of.

Far grinned at Mor. "No gifts for you?" he asked, the same way he told her he loved her.

Niels waited, excited to see what Far had planned.

Mor laughed. "Too naughty?" she guessed.

From behind a pillow — behind the exact pillow Mor sat against — Far pulled a flat package and set it in Mor's lap. "For you," he said, his voice suddenly deep.

She unwrapped it and held up an apron, for cooking.

She frowned, but it seemed like he was trying not to laugh. "Thank you," she said, and she *did* laugh, the words all bubbly and warm as they came out.

"Try it on," Far said.

Her eyebrows shot up; she put it on and twirled in it for him. It was a plain apron. Niels couldn't figure out what the joke was or what made it so special, but he did see she'd dropped a bracelet on the floor when she put the apron on.

Far picked it up. "What's this?" he teased. Niels could see it was made of little blue and white beads, to match the Delft pottery on display in this room.

Mor gasped happily and held her arm out for Far to put it on. "I love it."

"I love *you*," Far said.

Niels looked away before they got kissy gross again; love was everyday magic, it wasn't Jul magic.

2

TENSION

It was a Jul of tension.

The tree was only half-decorated, like someone had stood over it with a ladder and let ornaments hook wherever they landed. They hadn't gone to church to sing carols with the rest of the town.

Something was wrong. Niels didn't know what it was, except there had been a lot of screaming and crying by Mor, and Far went away for a few days and missed Niels. birthday. When Far got back there were even *more* fights, but these were the quiet kind of fights.

Quiet fights were scary, because no one would say what was wrong.

They were in the attic again, where they could hide. Mor was somewhere, Far...was he even home? Niels didn't know. He was afraid to ask. When he'd asked where Far went on his trip, all Mor did was burst into tears and later she told him Far had some important things to do in Copenhagen.

"What about the horses?" Cille cried out of the blue. Before then she had been playing contentedly with her set of toy dragons, which gave Niels the freedom to do his own thing while Viggo colored. "We forgot to feed them!"

They were supposed to feed the animals special treats today, for good luck next year. The old stories told of Nisse who would cause trouble if they didn't get treats today, but Niels knew they weren't true.

Cille didn't, though.

"I can take you outside," he said. He put down his workbook — First Class English — and his pen.

"I don't want to go outside," Viggo complained. "It's cold."

It was cold. Niels knew there were types of cold, though. He would rather deal with the cold outside than the cold in their house.

"Then don't go," Cille huffed. "I want to go."

Niels nodded, but he knew they couldn't leave Viggo inside alone. "Can you help me find carrots?" he asked Viggo. Involving him always worked better than telling him he had to help.

Viggo nodded, and they tiptoed out of the attic and into their bedrooms to change into heavier sweaters. From there, they made their way to the kitchen, to the refrigerator, to the carrots. "There aren't any apples," Niels apologized. There was probably grain somewhere in the stables, but he didn't know where.

"When are presents?" Viggo wanted to know.

Niels didn't have a clue. Maybe presents wouldn't happen this year. He hadn't seen any presents, not even the ones that weren't from Julemanden. No one had taken them on the big annual trip to do their Jul shopping in Herning.

"If you come to the stable," Niels pleaded, "you can have my bongos. Okay? We just have to be quiet."

He offered his hand to Viggo and waited.

Viggo took it. Niels let himself breathe. Now Cille wouldn't cry that the animals hadn't gotten their treats. He'd pulled it off, without anyone having to scream and bother his parents.

Once outside, they raced because it was okay to make noise in the yard. It *was* cold, so cold it made his lungs burn, and the air was crisp and clear. When he looked up over the car barn, he saw the aurora where it yawned endlessly and green into the dark night.

"Look!" he told Cille and Viggo. They ran across the yard with their faces up, watching the lights.

He hoped it was a sign that their lives would be okay.

In the stable doorway, they froze. Far leaned against one of the stalls, motionless and silent.

He didn't notice them come in.

They had the carrots. Niels *couldn't* turn around now, Cille would get angry and they'd fight and the situation would be worse.

He cleared his throat. Far didn't notice.

"Far," he said loudly, too loudly.

Far turned. It took a minute for his face to register they were there.

"Glædelig Jul?" Niels said, hopeful. At least Far was home, after all.

"Glædelig Jul," Far said back. He sounded sad, like he couldn't even find the energy to use his voice.

Viggo looked at Niels, and Niels shook his head. No hugging, not yet. Viggo was big on hugs, but Far...something was wrong.

Niels hid his hands in his pockets.

"Far," Viggo said. He went and hugged him anyway.

It was quiet in the stable, except one of the horses neighed.

Cille announced, "We're feeding the horses if you want to help. But you don't have to."

They waited. Finally, Far moved. "I'll help." He put his arm around Cille and hugged her against him on one side, while Viggo was on the other.

Niels' hands found their way further into his pockets. He was alone but that was okay; Cille and Viggo needed Far more.

"Glædelig Jul," Far said to each of them.

Niels followed them all deeper into the stable.

"I drew you a picture," Cille told Far. "It's a horse. It's purple and it has a lighter purple spot on its head. The spot is like a lavender-magenta-indigo kind of fuschia purple. It's in the attic."

Far laughed. "Thank you, Cille." He still sounded tired and sad.

He angled his head back so he could see Niels. "I'm sorry I missed your birthday."

He handed Niels a small, heavy package. It was the right size and weight that it might be what Niels most wanted for his birthday: A portable speaker system for his music player. "I already said it's okay," he promised Far. That was part of growing up, right? Your birthday didn't matter as much.

He wanted to ask Far where he'd gone, but he didn't want to ruin the present so he unwrapped it.

It wasn't speakers. It was a snow globe with a biplane inside it, and *Stauning Airshow* written on the front in English. When he twisted the knob on the bottom, the globe played the national anthem on a hidden music box while snow swirled around the plane.

Niels needed to cry, but crying felt like the most selfish thing he could do. He forced down the lump in his throat. "It's..." he tried to think of words that didn't sound ungrateful. "I like it."

He hated it. He tried not to, but what would he even do with it? Put it on a shelf and ignore it for the rest of his life?

He passed Far a carrot. "Did you have a good trip?"

Far sighed. "Eddie will move into our house."

Eddie was their cousin, but not really. Their fars were best friends. They'd gone to school together and gotten married the same year and Eddie was only a few months younger than Niels. Their families did almost everything together, whenever they could, even though Eddie and his far lived in Copenhagen and Niels lived in the middle of nowhere on the west coast of Denmark.

"Eddie?" Niels asked. He couldn't imagine Eddie living with them. Would he sleep in Niels' room? Or would they empty out one of the other bedrooms for him, one of the ones nobody used because they were filled with antiques and family heirlooms? "Is that why Mor is mad?"

"Part of it," Far said. His eyes were on one of the horses as he fed it. "Not at Eddie. She is excited for Eddie."

Wait, was he here already?

Viggo realized at the same time. "Where is he?" he asked. "Let's go!" He lobbed a carrot into one of the stalls and ran toward the door.

"*Is* he here?" Niels asked.

He could show Eddie his snowglobe. They could hang out in his room and listen to the national anthem instead of good music, and watch the snow settle.

Niels wasn't being fair. Something was wrong. It wasn't Far's fault that whatever had gone wrong had happened right now.

"He's inside," Far said. He called Viggo back, and suddenly he was more firm, more himself. All of the faded-out sadness was gone. Most of it, anyway, maybe some of it was still there in the way his shoulders sagged and his eyes didn't gleam like usual. "The horses," he scolded Viggo, "don't like when you throw things at them. Be nice. They are our friends."

"I'm being very nice," Cille told him. "All the horses love me."

He rubbed the top of her head. "Thank you, Cille. There's a new horse coming...it also couldn't arrive in time. Your mother wanted to give it to you."

"A horse?" Cille's whole face was bright. "For me?"

Far nodded, and Cille clapped her hands and ran to find it a stall. Viggo ran off with her.

Niels looked at Far. "Is Eddie moving here because his far died?"

Eddie's mor died early last spring. They'd all gone to Eddie's house in Copenhagen for two whole weeks, for the funeral and to help Eddie's far take care of all the finances. Eddie's little sister Alma had died too, but no one ever told Niels how.

He bet Eddie knew.

Far put his hand on Niels' shoulder and looked into his eyes. He took a deep breath and stepped away from Niels. "No, but his far is sick."

What did Far almost say? What was the secret?

"Will he live here too?" Niels asked. Cille and Viggo were back now — they probably heard Eddie's far was sick. They watched Far too, waiting for an answer.

Viggo shivered, and Far didn't answer. He lifted Viggo up onto his hip. "Let's get inside."

Niels bet Eddie's far, Edvard, was moving in too. It explained all the anger. "Is *that* why Mor is mad?"

"Yes," Far said like a sigh. "It is."

That was easy. Mor would calm down after a few days, and — "We can make him better and he can go home and we can be happy again." Like they used to be, like last Jul.

Far laughed. "Maybe," he said, the way he said maybe when he really meant *no but I don't want to have this argument.*

Edvard was *really* sick. Eddie would live with them forever, probably.

Mor would calm down though. She always got mad about things and then calmed down later. Niels felt like he'd held his breath for a long time and now he could finally breathe again.

"Will we catch his cold?" Cille asked. She slid her hand into Far's like she wasn't scared of the tension.

"No," Far promised. "You're safe."

He picked Cille up too, so he had Cille and Viggo each in one arm. Niels walked next to him, back under the aurora and into the house.

Eddie was there. He sat on the old church pew in the entryway and looked about as miserable as Niels felt.

Viggo kicked and made himself heavy until Far put him down. As soon as his feet hit the stone floor he ran toward Eddie, screaming his name.

Eddie looked at Niels. "Hej."

"Hej," Niels said.

They could hear tight voices from the gold room just through the arched doorway, tense but polite. It was Mor and Edvard.

"Will Alma live here too?" Cille asked.

Far cringed, because Alma was dead and Cille had forgotten. Eddie got quieter somehow, even though he hadn't said much; he got smaller and weaker right in front of them.

Nobody answered Cille, because now Mor stood in the doorway. Edvard was still in the gold room.

"Maybe you will have a girl?" Far asked Mor.

"Maybe," she said, and she managed not to move her face at all.

A baby? Maybe *that* was the problem. "You're pregnant?" Niels asked her.

She smoothed her skirt. "I'm not sure yet. We'll see."

Like Eddie, Far wilted.

Everyone was quiet, too quiet. Niels' hands wanted to go back in his pockets again, but he was afraid if he moved everyone would look at him. He stood there with his palms flat against the sides of his thighs and waited for someone else to do something.

Far finally moved. All of them breathed out at once, and they followed him to the blue room where the sad tree sat.

There were no presents under it, but Far walked to a table under a window and picked up a few wrapped items. He passed one to each kid, even to Eddie.

Cille looked at the tree, her eyes glassy with tears. "Where are all the ones from Julemanden?"

Julemanden wasn't real.

Niels remembered last year, Far dressed as Julemanden in the kitchen. He had wondered if Julemanden was real or only a story, and Far had given him one last magical Jul.

Cille did not have that. Niels couldn't fix it for her, no one could. Even Viggo...he was five years old...he would find out this year.

Eddie opened his present first, which was brave of him. It was a paint set, the kind in the office aisle at the grocery store. "Thanks," Eddie said in a quiet voice. He hugged their parents, almost more obligatory than warm.

Niels' breath caught.

He steadied it.

As oldest kid in the family, he should go next. He didn't want to know what was under the wrapping paper. He probably would cry, if it was another snow globe. It didn't feel like one; it felt small and bendy.

He opened it. Inside, he found a watch with an antique silver band and a face with all kinds of circles and symbols on it, not a regular watch face. The curved glass caught the light from the chandelier as Niels looked at it.

His eyes darted to Far's wrist. A faint tan line showed where the watch used to be — the aviator watch that had been in their family since World War II. It had a new strap...the old one had been leather...but this watch...

Suddenly the Stauning Airshow snow globe made sense. Niels could see it: He loved airplanes, they lived *right* near an airport, he already had an aviator watch...he would be a pilot when he grew up.

He checked with Far first. "I can really have it?"

"It's for you," Far promised. He patted Niels' shoulder. "You are growing up."

But it was Far's watch. For forever.

He didn't know what *else* was wrong, but he knew Far giving him this watch was bad. It was supposed to be his watch until he died, and then it would go to Niels or Viggo. That was...it was the rules.

This watch had a new strap because the old strap had been stained with Niels' grandfather's blood. The whole family knew the story of how he'd crashed one of the family's cars, killing himself and Niels' grandmother, and almost killing Niels.

His grandfather, Cide, had worn the watch until he died.

Niels pressed it against his chest now.

Maybe it was nothing. Maybe Far meant it; he was growing up.

He nodded. An unexpected smile crept across his face and he held up the snow globe. "I'm going to be an aviator!"

He could imagine flying in planes, maybe fixing up a biplane with Far, keeping it in the car barn, even *flying* it in the airshow someday.

Mor pressed her lips together. "Take care of that, Niels." She didn't mean the snow globe.

"I will," he promised. Owning it scared him more than anything he'd ever owned, even his toy sword. He would take care of it. He'd never let anything happen to it, ever. Forever.

Far looked at Mor. "I told Cille what her present is while we were in the barn."

Mor nodded. She didn't make eye contact with Far like they usually did, all warm and always two seconds from kissing. Today her eyes stayed on the collar of his shirt and she looked like maybe she would never kiss him again.

"Well," Mor cleared her throat. "I had gotten her a little thing too. So she would have something to open today." She handed a gift to Cille, who tore it open eagerly.

It was a bracelet with beads that looked like the Delft pottery in the room.

It was the same one Far got Mor last year for Jul. Niels didn't have the bracelet memorized; that wasn't how he knew it was the same. He knew because of the way Far sat on the couch, angled away from Mor, even more wilted than he was in the hall.

He knew because of the way Mor said, "Well I had to give her *something*!"

Nobody said anything while Cille slipped the bracelet over her wrist. It was too big, like the aviator watch was probably too big for Niels.

There was something there, a metaphor, but Niels pushed the thought away.

"What did Julemanden get me?" Viggo asked.

Nothing, was what Julemanden got him. Julemanden didn't exist and their family was falling apart.

Mor passed Viggo a small package: He unwrapped it to find a small fossil, the imprint left by a fish's bones.

Viggo gaped at it in shock. "I was bad!" he cried. "This is worse than coal!"

He ran out of the room and Mor ran after him.

Niels had a million questions: How did Viggo know about the American Santa's coal tradition; why was everyone so upset, and what weren't they telling him; what did the watch mean; why was Edvard here, but not doing the Jul presents with them?

Niels met Far's eyes, more firm. He had a right to know what all of this was. He was almost an adult, at nine. "Are you divorcing? Is that...is Mor marrying Edvard?"

Eddie was suddenly busy with some of the strands of silver on the tree.

"She is not marrying Edvard," Far assured him.

But he hadn't said anything about the divorce.

What would happen? Would Mor stay here and garden, and Far would move to their house in Copenhagen? Would they ever see him?

"Why?" he asked.

"Because," Cille said. "He kissed a boy. And now Mor and Far can't be friends anymore."

"So? Lots of boys kiss each other." The only reason Niels hadn't kissed Eddie's cheek today was because everything felt wrong. Maybe it was mean, but Niels wasn't really happy to see him.

"Not like *that*," Cille said, and she made kissy face at him like when their parents kissed.

Niels looked sharply at Far. He'd kissed a boy? Like Freddie Mercury.

"No, Cille," Far said gently, but his eyes were on Niels. "I love your mother." He passed out a plastic tray of store-bought krebinetter and klejner. "It's time to be happy, not worry."

He sounded too worried to even say those words.

Freddie Mercury kissed a boy and he'd *died*. Not right away, but he'd died.

But Edvard had been kissing a boy all year. Niels had heard his parents talk about how Edvard had a new boyfriend during the summer. And Edvard was still alive.

Edvard was sick.

Freddie Mercury had been sick.

What if Far had kissed Edvard? What if he was sick too?

"Are *you* sick?" Niels asked.

"No," Far said. He put his hands in his pockets.

Niels had a klejner. He hated how perfect the store ones were. When Mor made them, they were always uneven and some of them were sticks instead of diamonds. Every one of these klejner was the same.

This was what he decided: Edvard was sick, and he would die like Freddie Mercury, so Eddie would move in with them *now* so they could adopt him when his far died. And Edvard would need help, especially when he got sicker, which was why Mor was so mad at Far.

Everything made sense.

He ate another klejner and watched Mor chase Viggo into the room. She sighed at Far. "Now he wants *another* fossil so the fish can play together."

Far laughed and tousled Viggo's hair. "I think we can find you one."

Before Niels' grandparents died, they had collected artifacts from all over the world. Two rooms of Falkhus were full of their collection, including fossils.

"Is Edvard going to die?" Niels whispered to Far. He wanted to know if his guess was right. "Like Freddie Mercury?"

Far looked across the room, where Eddie watched them from next to the Jul tree. He looked at all the kids. "He is sick, but we will try to help him."

Mor sat on the couch and slid her arm behind Far's back. "But he will be sick for a long time. So he and Eddie," she smiled to Eddie, "will stay here where we can help them."

"And you can play all the time," Far said. "And go to school together."

They started playing, because it felt almost like an order: We have told you what is going on, so now you must be happy and play. Far brought another fossil and Niels showed Eddie the snow globe and they painted together while they talked about what kind of biplane they wanted to buy when they were older.

Niels only looked up once, to see his parents with their heads bowed together. "Whatever happens," Mor promised Far, "I love you."

Far kissed her cheek, tears in his eyes. "I love you," he whispered back.

It was real magic, the kind that fixed everything.

3

AMBIVALENCE

It was a Jul of ambivalence.

Surrounded by happy churchgoers, by candles and smoke and a roaring organ, Niels leaned into his sister Cille. She had asked to be on the outside this time so she could watch the procession of singers when they came up the aisle.

On his other side was Eddie, dressed in an outfit almost identical to Niels': Collared blue and white shirt, maroon sweater, dress slacks. Niels and Mor had argued about the slacks before church: Niels only got ten days off from school, where his uniform required dress slacks every day, and he'd told her he had no intention of wearing them on a day he didn't have to.

She'd told him church was *not* a day he didn't have to.

That was why Eddie and Viggo stood between them now: Mor was way down at the other end of the pew where her opinions and Niels' opinions wouldn't clash.

He bet she wouldn't have even noticed if he hadn't said anything. She liked them all quiet, behaved, and stress-free.

The organist started a new hymn: Lovely Is the Blue Sky. They sang about waving from Earth up to the stars, and tears inexplicably filled Niels' eyes.

It wasn't about the jeans; he knew it wasn't. It was that he only got ten days home with Far before he had to go back to boarding school, and Far hadn't come to church. Niels wanted to stay home, but he'd made it about the jeans instead and now he and Mor were fighting.

When Far died, when Edvard died...would they be in the stars? Would they see them waving?

Niels ducked out of the pew and made his way to the men's room, half-blinded by tears. He didn't want to sing a stupid song about a guiding star leading them home to God. Faith in God was as pointless as faith in Julemanden...made-up stories to help people feel good about all the despair in the world.

Niels stared at himself in the mirror. He didn't look much like Far, not really. He was always tense, and his nose was jagged like Bedstefar Cide's nose; Far was almost always relaxed and he had a nice normal-looking nose.

He only had ten days, and he'd already used up two of them. Today was almost over and then he would only have seven days left to see Far before the end of term.

What if Far died when Niels was at school? Would he even see him again?

No, that wouldn't happen. He was still healthy, most of the time, just tired and thin.

Niels splashed water on his eyes to hide the crying, and straightened. He was the biggest brother. He would do this. It was Jul. He had to be happy. It was every kid's job to be happy today of all days.

He forced a smile on his face. He knew it was there because he practiced it sometimes in the mirror to make sure he'd smile when Far needed it, or when Cille or Viggo did.

He walked back into the church like everything was fine, and joined his family. He was back in time to have to sing about the guiding star, but he forced his way through it.

He kind of numbed himself to the rest of the songs, until church was over. He numbed his way through leaving — through listening to Cille talk about how much she wanted to be in the church procession next year, through people hugging them all and asking after Far when these were people they only even talked to once a year *at church.*

Mor's answer was the same to all of them: "Oh, wouldn't you know, we have a squirrel infestation in the attic and of course they found a way into the house just as we were getting Viggo dressed to come to church!"

As if Viggo couldn't dress himself; as if people didn't know Far was sick; as if there was something to be embarrassed about.

They got in the car. For a moment before Mor started the engine, everything was quiet.

She looked at Niels. "It would help," she said, "if you didn't look so surly all the time. And what were you thinking? Leaving in the middle of church!"

He looked at her for a whole gaping minute. "I went to the bathroom," he told her.

"You couldn't hold it? Everyone saw you go."

No, everyone didn't see him go. Nobody even cared.

He looked out the window, at all the happy families talking in the snow. "I hate you," he said.

Mor huffed. "You could try concealing that fact until you go back to school," she suggested. "For your father's sake."

She started the car and eased it onto the road. He leaned his head against the side window, watching fields of snow fly behind the half-fogged glass. This would be the rest of his life, forever; let's pretend everything is perfect, for Far. They never fought in front of him or Edvard, never argued with Mor where they could hear, never complained.

It was fake.

Mor pulled the car onto their lane and into the car barn. Someone was there to take the car. They would clean it, refuel it, make sure it was ready for the next time Mor wanted to drive it.

Mor said they were lucky to have a big estate, to have money for boarding school, to have help with every part of their lives.

Niels would have traded all of it to have their lives normal again, to have Far healthy. He wanted to be home, but home was gone; different.

All the lights at the front of the house were lit as they crossed the lawn to the front door. It looked incongruous. The whole day, the whole *season* was incongruous with reality. It was too warm and happy and perfect.

Inside, they found Far standing in the blue room next to an enormous Jul tree, bigger than they had ever had before, lit and decorated in shimmery strands of silver.

Edvard stood behind him, angled away from them as they all came into the room.

Under the tree, piled higher than even the charity tree at church, was a mountain of presents.

"Glædelig Jul!" Far and Edvard yelled as they walked in.

This was to make up for last Jul, for the fossils and the watch. Niels was positive about it. He couldn't help the grin that spread across his face. "Do we get to sing again this year?" he asked.

He knew Far had cancer. Not just cancer, but *defining* cancer, whatever that meant. As far as Niels could tell, it meant Far somehow looked thinner and developed a potbelly at the same time. His neck and face were puffy too.

What it really meant was Far was tired more often, and his parents were sad, and Edvard — even though he got sick first — was actually healthier than Far.

It meant that if Far had set all of this up, he would need to rest. Soon.

But for now, when Niels asked Far if they would sing again, Far only grinned and bellowed the first few lyrics to *Jul det Cool*. They all joined in, through probably a dozen songs since Far had missed church. Eddie sat at the grand piano and played insanely fancy versions of each song, harmonizing with them as they sang.

And then it was over.

Far passed Niels an envelope set at the very top of the pile. "For you and Eddie to share," he said.

Eddie stood next to Niels as he tore the envelope open. He bet it was spending money for school, because on weekends they got to go into the city as a group and go shopping. He glanced at Eddie, excited. The things they could buy with a generous donation...

It wasn't cash or even a check: It was a photograph of a full recording studio set up somewhere stone.

This was...they...did Far want to take him somewhere to play music? To record music?

He looked up. "Wow," he joked. "Thanks. A picture."

Far laughed. "It wouldn't fit under the tree. It's down in the cellar, everything you need to make your own music."

Holy shit.

No, not holy shit, he wasn't allowed to say that anywhere except the school dorms.

He patted Eddie's back. "We can write stuff. We can *make* stuff!"

Last summer, they'd played together a ton: Far on second guitar, Edvard on bass, Eddie on the drums, and Niels on lead guitar. They'd played almost every day, mostly doing Queen covers and some of the crappy 80s songs...Billy Idol, A-ha, Duran Duran. A-ha had been a favorite because they were Norwegian which was closer to Denmark than most bands. Niels pushed Metallica because they *were* Danish, but Far and Edvard didn't seem to like that sound as much.

Eddie tossed his head back and groaned. "You want to be loud, don't you," he complained, but he laughed too.

Niels bumped into him. "That's what it's for. Right, Far?"

Far laughed and made eye contact with Edvard. Happy. He was really happy, all the way to his eyes, not just pretending. "You should be loud," he encouraged.

Viggo stepped between Niels and the fars, with a present in his hands. "This one's for me!" he said. He tore the paper off in a frenzy. "It's a..."

"It's an ocarina," Far told him. He showed him how to place his fingers, where to blow.

Viggo turned the music lesson into a hug. Far picked him up and carried him over to the couch and sat, and Niels had a feeling he wouldn't budge again until it was time for rice pudding.

Far looked at Cille. "There was a great argument about your present."

Her face lit up, with a look of doubt toward Mor. "Is it bad?" she asked, hopeful. "Is it something Mor will hate?"

"Very much," Far promised. He nodded toward an enormous box to one side of the pile. All of them watched quietly while Cille opened it and pulled out book after book, with titles like, *Real Monsters of Human History* and *Theories on Jack the Ripper* and even one in Italian, *Il Mostro di Firenze.*

Cille hugged Far. Still hugging her, he said, "We know you love monsters..."

"Can I read at the table?" she asked. She had *Il Mostro di Firenze* tucked under her arm.

"Just this once," Mor said. "And I don't want to hear any details about the murders."

Cille nodded. "I promise."

Niels passed a heavy gift for Far. It was the only thing he'd gotten him: It was a safe with a false combination lock on the front, and a real lock hidden behind a secret latch. He'd built it at school, after Edvard had his wallet stolen at the hospital in Stauning. Eddie had made one for Edvard too, so their fars could keep their things safe in the hospital.

Niels showed Far how to open the real combination lock. "There's a button under the lip," he said. "I made the combination my birthday, but you can change it."

Far closed it and reset the lock before trying it himself. "Your birthday is perfect," he said. He hugged Niels.

This was one of the last hugs. Far smelled like cigars and medicine. It was as incongruous as the Jul lights while their fars were dying.

Aggressive cancer. Months, the doctors had said. Maybe a year. This hug...Far felt so solid and fine. How could he be dying? How could they be running out of time with him?

Far leaned forward, shifting Niels away from the hug. "Mor?" Far asked.

Edvard sat down on his other side and put his arm around Far's back. Not like friends, but like Far and Mor used to sit.

Far passed a gift to Mor. When she opened it, there was a CD and earrings taped to the cover. "I made it," Far told her, about the CD.

Mor nodded and glanced at Edvard. "We'll listen later?" she suggested. She stood. "I'll get the pudding ready. Go ahead and open gifts without me," and she raced out of the room so fast that even though Far called her back, she didn't hear it.

"I'll get her," Niels offered, even though he bet he'd get stuck setting the table instead. He left, but not before he saw Edvard kiss Far full on the mouth, also not like friends.

Niels stumbled in the hall, confused. Far and Mor, when they'd explained that Far was sick, had said this: That Edvard had hurt himself and Far saved him, and the disease had passed from Edvard to Far through a cut in Far's hand, through touching Edvard's blood.

It was a lie.

Far and Edvard were *together*.

He'd gotten sick the same way Freddie Mercury did. He'd picked...he'd picked Edvard over their family, he'd picked dying over living, he'd picked...he'd...

Niels all but ran to the kitchen, blinded by tears for the second time in one night, but he froze outside the kitchen door. A strangled, muffled sound came from inside the kitchen. He peeked around the corner and saw Mor crouched behind the big stove, holding a towel against her own mouth while she screamed into it.

Niels went to the stove and poured some tea from the kettle. He knelt by Mor and set the cup in her hand. "It's okay," he told her even though it wasn't.

She swallowed back her tears. "Niels." She sipped the tea and unscrunched her legs, relaxing more against the wall.

"What happened?" Niels asked. She hadn't seen the kiss. "Do you hate the CD?"

Mor laugh-cried. "I hate that it's a goodbye gift. Songs for me, maybe even words for me, when he's gone." She looked at Niels. "And...I struggle to feel charitable toward Edvard sometimes."

Niels did too. He sat down next to her with a cup of warm tea nestled in his hands. "So you scream into a towel? Does it help?"

She laughed. "More than screaming at him, I think." She shifted so she was angled more toward him. "Anyway, it's Jul. What else did you find under the tree?"

He wasn't a little kid anymore. He didn't want Mor and Far to lie to him about their lives. "I saw Edvard and Far kissing."

Mor stared into the kitchen for a long time. He waited. While he waited, he studied her face. She had his jagged nose, but on her it was perfect. Maybe Far didn't like it, though, or maybe he didn't like how mad she got when she was angry. Edvard was almost never mad.

Mor looked at him finally. "Yes. They are together. They are in love."

Her face broke when she said the last part, crumbled into pieces Niels didn't know how to fix. Even though she was crying, even though she couldn't even hold her own face together, she reached out and held Niels' cheeks between her palms. "You must promise me something."

He waited.

"Do you love your father?"

Of course he did. They had both taught him that love was love no matter what. His father was still his father, even if he kissed Edvard. He was still the same him, the one Niels had always loved.

"Ja," he said.

She nodded. "Then you must be happy for him. You must never show your confusion or your hurt or your misery. The happier he is, the healthier his body will be and the more time he will have here. We will have our own time to grieve later…" she trailed off, her face a scrumpled mess of redness and tears. She shuddered. "Grieving is a process, and today I am experiencing grief in the form of anger. At Edvard."

He thought about that, about all his emotions he hadn't known what to do with lately. Was *that* what it was? He'd thought it must be something embarrassing like puberty, but maybe it was grief.

"We will play music in the cellar later," he told her. He looked at his hands. Maybe he shouldn't admit this to her. She might not want to know it; might be better off thinking he was happy when he played. If he told her music was where he sent his anger, she would *always* know, and any time he played...

Ja. He needed her to be happy too, for the same reason she needed Far to be happy. Mor might not be sick like Far, but she wasn't well either.

Instead he said, "You should tell Edvard how you feel. Whenever we fight at school they make us talk."

Mor studied his face. "Does it help?"

Not really. "Every time."

She laughed. She didn't believe him.

"Well..." he said. "Where will Eddie go when his far dies?"

"Why should he go anywhere?" she asked.

"Because...you're mad at his far?"

She sighed and ran her fingers through his hair. "I am angry with him, but I also love him like a brother, and love is not-"

"I know," he interrupted. She quoted that sonnet at him for most of his childhood, telling him she would always love him no matter what. "Love is not love that alters when it alteration finds."

"Yes." She smoothed her skirt and stood, before offering her hand to help him up. "He will live here and be family, and we will look after him for as long as we can, just as we are doing for Far." She ran her thumbs under his eyes and wiped away the wetness. The salt stung his cheeks as it dried. "Now." She wiped her own tears away too. "We will be happy, yes?"

"Yes," he promised. "For Far."

He helped her set the table in the small dining room, helped her spoon the rice pudding into bowls. He didn't even look to see whose bowl had the almond in it. He hoped it was in Far's bowl and Far would get the treat.

They called the others in from the blue room and sat finally. Niels hadn't opened a single present except for that envelope, but he didn't care. No one else seemed to either.

He turned to Far while they ate. "Can you make a CD with all of us?"

Maybe Far would be too tired, but maybe it would be a good distraction for him. Playing music would help Niels be happy too; he wouldn't have to pretend.

Far shared a smile with Edvard. "We can get started after we eat."

Edvard nodded his agreement.

"Not the Nissemand song," Eddie groaned. "Do we have to do that one?"

He might as well ask if they had to have a tree at Jul. "We have to do that one," Niels insisted.

"We do the Nissemand, then you can pick the next?" Far suggested.

They debated a playlist for a while and finally settled on one that was a mix of Jul music and some of their favorite songs from last summer. Viggo watched with an expression that fell somewhere between hopeful and resigned.

Niels remembered the feeling of Mor's hands on his cheeks, calling him into focus. "Just once," he told Viggo. Tonight was about family, about together.

"I'm done eating!" Viggo declared. He set his spoon down with a *clink* and pushed his chair back from the table.

"No one has found the almond yet," Mor protested.

Cille, who had been quiet since coming into the dining room, blushed. "I did. I wanted Far to find it, so I put it back in the bowl and didn't say anything."

She'd put the almond *back*? Had it been in her mouth?

Niels gazed at her with all the disgust her statement deserved. He refused to eat another bite of pudding.

"The treat is for you, Cille," Far insisted. "You found it."

Tears welled in her eyes. "I don't want it."

Far sighed and pulled the pudding bowl so it sat between them. He held a spoon out toward her. "Will you help me find it?"

She fished around in the pudding for her salivated-on almond. When she found it, Far held it up and looked at Mor. "I've found it!"

He hugged Cille against his side. "Where is my prize?" he asked Mor. It was almost his usual flirty tone.

Before Mor could answer, Edvard teased him: "You'll have to bribe me for it. Cille found it first."

Far ran his fingers over the back of Edvard's neck and under his chin. He looked like he might kiss him right there at the table. "Please, may I have the treat? To share with the kids."

Edvard *did* kiss him.

Niels met Mor's eyes down the length of the table. She mouthed *hygge* at him and plastered a smile on her face.

Hygge wasn't happiness, exactly. It was being at peace, being content, being everything their family wasn't.

He nodded.

"We should all play and sing," Eddie said, his eyes on Cille. "I can't play keyboard *and* drums, and I know you like to hit things."

Everyone laughed. Niels wished he had been the one to break the tension, but he reminded himself that what mattered was that Far and Edvard and Mor were all laughing now as they passed out the chocolate skildpadder that were Far's favorite candy.

"Food, first," Far said. He snapped his arm out without warning and caught Viggo trying to sneak toward the cellar. He hooked him back toward the table and offered him a second skildpadder. "We eat together as a family," he told Viggo firmly.

Ja. They pretended together as a family too.

4

DESPAIR

It was a Jul of despair.

Edvard had died in August, with an unexpected case of pneumonia that turned into a full-body infection from his medication IV thing in his chest. Niels didn't really know the details. He only knew Edvard was dead just three days after being diagnosed with pneumonia, and now Eddie was an orphan.

Far was mostly bedridden. He had made the decision to stop treatment and now, according to him and Mor, it was only a matter of time.

This would be the last Jul with Far. In the few weeks since autumn break, Far had deteriorated visibly. His skin was yellow and waxy with weird dark blotches. He was thin. Even his neck, which had been swollen for so long, looked thin and frail. His eyes were sunken, and he slept more than half of every day.

They had set up the Jul tree in the green room, because that was where Far's bed and IV and monitors were. It was a less-drafty room, which was good because Far was prone to cold sweats while he slept.

When he woke late in the afternoon, all of them assembled near the tree. Far moved from his bed to the loveseat, sitting upright to watch Jul with all of them.

He had the button in his hand, the one that gave him pain medicine through his IV whenever he pressed it. The IV also kept him hydrated, which was good because he barely ate or drank anything.

"Happy Jul," Far said. He coughed and cleared his throat and said it again; better; louder.

Niels passed him a mug of fresh-brewed tea.

"Thank you," he said. He set it on the end table without taking a sip. "Let's see what you all got this year."

"Is there something you'll eat?" Niels begged. He knew he was supposed to pretend to be happy, and he'd done a good job of that all year, but it was *over*. Pretending hadn't saved Far; nothing would.

"I'm okay," Far insisted, but when Viggo climbed onto the loveseat next to Far and passed him a skildpadder, Far did force it down. "Thank you," he told Viggo between bites. "My favorite."

Thank Christ he ate something, even if it had no nutritional value. It took him endless minutes to eat it and somehow that little bit of chewing made him look more tired. He shifted on the loveseat, leaned back more, his elbow on the armrest. "What did you all get for Jul?"

"I don't want to open anything," Viggo said. He had his arms folded across his chest, a dare to anyone who tried to argue.

"Me neither," Niels and Cille said at the same time.

Their eyes met and both of them almost laughed, except laughing felt so so wrong right now.

"Why not?" Far asked. He looked between all of them. The pain on his face...emotional more than physical...told them he knew. "It's Jul."

Niels squeezed Eddie's hand; he didn't have to say it, that opening his presents without Edvard felt as wrong as opening presents while Far suffered.

"Because," Niels said to Far. "We can always get presents. Can't we...sing or something?"

Far deflated. "Sing for me?"

"No," Viggo insisted. "I want to sing together."

Niels knelt next to him, which made Viggo taller for once. "I'll sing with you," he said. He looked up at Mor, pleading with his eyes. He couldn't do this alone, he couldn't make it happy when it wasn't.

"We'll all sing," Mor said. She rested her hand on Viggo's shoulder and hugged Cille against her.

They sang, Nissemand of course. It might have been the worst song they could have sung, all about how unfair it was that elves had to work on Christmas while everyone got the day off. The song was true in a brutal, unyielding way.

All of them were crying by the time the song was done, even Far. They ended up on the loveseat, all of them snuggled: Viggo sat on Far's lap, and Cille was tucked against his side, with Mor next to her. Niels and Eddie sat on the floor in front of Far.

They sat like that, caught in an infinite moment they could never hold.

Far coughed and broke the spell.

Niels looked up at him from the floor. "Can we camp in here tonight?" He left off the *with you* because he figured that was implied.

Far looked at Mor, then back to Niels. "You can if you open your presents."

Christ. That was a good one. Niels narrowed his eyes. "If you drink your tea."

For a second he thought he saw a spark of amusement in Far's eyes, but it faded so quickly that it might not have been there at all. Far sighed and took a long sip of tea. He nodded toward the presents.

Niels kept his promise. Slowly. First he and the other kids sorted the presents into piles by who they went to. He and Eddie found a set that looked identical, one for him and one for Eddie, and they opened that first.

Each of them had gotten matching model airplanes, perfect miniatures of an Airbus a330, first flight in 1992, three engine options although they obviously weren't included in the model versions.

"What do you think?" Far asked them both. He passed Eddie a card. "Edvard helped pick it out on our last trip to Stauning. He wrote this for you while he was in hospital."

Eddie opened the card and read in silence. When he finished

reading, he tucked the card into his back pocket and hugged the plane against himself.

"You picked these out together?" Niels asked.

Far nodded. "We did."

He wondered if there would be two sets of presents this year — one from Mor and one from Far — or whether they had collaborated.

He wondered what all the airplane gifts over the years meant. "Do you want me to be a pilot?"

Far tilted his head, surprised. "I want you to be anything you want to be."

That was nice and vague. Niels could really get a lot of mileage out of that when he was sixteen and trying to decide whether to be done with school.

"Did *you* want to be a pilot?" Niels asked.

Far leaned toward him. "Niels. I want you to know there are no limits. No places too far, no dreams too big, for you."

Anything. Far was saying he could do anything. Niels nodded.

"And me?" Cille asked.

"The same." Far smiled at her. "Except maybe not a murderer."

Cille and Mor both laughed, and then, serious, Cille asked, "An investigator?"

"If you like, yes," Far told her. He hugged her.

Viggo climbed back onto Far's lap. "And me?"

He was still a little kid. Far tilted his head back and ruffled Viggo's hair. "What do you want?"

"I don't know yet," Viggo said. He started to cry.

Far hugged him against his chest and let him sob for a minute. "You can be anything, then," Mor promised. "Just like Niels and Cille."

"Okay," Viggo said, muffled by Far's shirt.

They were quiet again. No one had opened any more presents; no one wanted to. Far hadn't drunk any more of his tea, either.

Niels pushed the airplane away, off his lap and toward the mountain of gifts that could never buy Far's health. "I don't want to pretend anymore," he said. He knew his tone was surly, almost defiant.

He waited for Mor to call him into the other room to tell him off, but she only looked down at her hands.

"Pretend what?" Far asked.

"That you're not dying," Viggo told him. He touched Far's cheek, the stubble there, and circled the shadows under his eyes. "You're going to die."

That was a small part of it, and Viggo knew it. Niels added, "That *we're* okay. That we can even pretend to be happy right now."

Mor's head collapsed into her hands, her face hidden from view.

Far sighed, his breath shaky before it caught in a cough. When he could breathe well enough to talk he reached out and held Niels' hand. "You'll be happy again. I'm sorry for this." He looked at Mor. "Maybe it would be best if I lived somewhere else, so the kids don't have to see this."

"No!" Niels bellowed before Far even finished the thought. He looked at Mor and poured all of his persuasive energy into this one moment: "Please don't make me go back to school."

His parents shared a look.

Far looked at Niels again, searching his face. "You want to be here, through this?"

"Please." He had weeks left, at best. Niels didn't want to spend them learning Latin declensions and practicing oration. He wanted to be with Far for as long as he could be, and he didn't want Viggo and Cille here alone with Mor when Far died.

"You can stay," Far said.

"Both of us?" Eddie asked him, and Far nodded again

Far took another sip of tea and closed his eyes for a moment. "Presents," he ordered. He opened his eyes and looked at all of them, even Mor. "I will not leave you, no matter where I go."

"We won't leave you either," Cille promised. "No matter where." She picked up an awkwardly heavy present that turned out to be a forensic chemistry set.

Niels and the others set to work on unwrapping their gifts while Far lay on the loveseat. Through it all he heard Mor and Cille arguing — no, Cille could *not* perform autopsies on any future dead family pets — and Far coughing, and Viggo shouting in excitement about his nerf guns, which he proceeded to shoot at all of them until Mor finally told him to only target ornaments on the tree.

After presents, they sang Jul hymns at the piano. They got to *Lovely Is the Blue Sky*, singing, "When the star so light and gentle let itself be seen by midnight," when Far's machine across the room began to beep a panicked tattoo.

Eddie hesitated, his fingers frozen tense over the black and ivory piano keys.

Mor squeezed all of them against her and they restarted the song, louder over the beeping: "Lovely is the blue sky; bright it is to look at; how the golden stars twinkle; how they smile, how they wave."

5

RAGE

It was a Jul of rage.

Niels and Eddie sat in the headmaster's office. Mor sat beside them. She smoothed her skirt and leveled her outraged stare on Niels. "I cannot *believe* I had to fly home from Cascais for this!"

"Maybe, if you can't believe it, it's a fairy tale," he suggested. He needed to shield Eddie from most of this; it had been Niels' idea, Niels' money, Niels' words that convinced the rest of the boys to help.

Mor's eyes contracted in fury. "A *fairy tale*?"

"Ja, like...you know...hard to believe because it's not real."

She huffed and her nostrils flared, but he suspected she was trying not to laugh. She crossed her legs at the ankle. "Please refrain from suggesting to Headmaster Bjelke that it was all a hallucination."

He hadn't even thought of that. It would only add to the promise of expulsion, which Niels looked forward to with relish. It was Jul, not a time to be trapped at school. "Why couldn't we go to Cascais with you?"

Mor glanced at Cille and Viggo, where they sat on a bench in the back of Bjelke's office. Cille was reading and Viggo had a portable game system in his hands and earbuds to tune out the sound in the room. "I thought it might be easier with them, if they could imagine that Far was with the two of you and I was with the two of them."

That was ridiculous. They'd all been there last year when Far died. It wasn't news, it wasn't shocking. The best way to survive this Jul was *together*, not in different countries. And what part of the beaches at Cascais would feel right or familiar to Cille and Viggo?

Before he could point any of that out, Bjelke opened the door from his inner sanctum office Niels had never seen the interior of, thank Christ, and stepped into the outer office. He smiled at Mor, reminded her who he was in case she somehow forgot, and opened a file folder filled with complaints about Niels' behavior. The stack was at least three centimeters thick.

Niels smiled at a job well done.

Bjelke sat in his Brazilian cherry-wood swivel chair and studied the top paper in the stack.

"We have tried to be patient with him, Baronesse. Especially given the tragedies your family has faced, but...it is simply too much." He straightened his already straight papers.

"How have you tried?" Mor asked.

"What?"

"How have you tried? He has lost both of his fathers in the space of a year. What have you done to make this easier for him?"

Bjelke sighed. "I see you intend this to be an interesting discussion." He unstraightened his stack of papers. "Since autumn break alone, he has: Been caught with hard liquor four times. His marks have slipped in every class save oration, where he incited what can only be described as a small student riot. He has released animals into the administrative building on three separate occasions: chickens, pigeons, and pigs." Bjelke met Mor's eyes. "Yesterday, he and Eddie and four other students in their class stole a school van and drove to Rigshospitalet without permission."

Mor interrupted before Bjelke could add to that list: "I certainly hope he didn't steal the school van *with* permission."

Bjelke narrowed his eyes at her.

"Further," Mor said now that she had his full, disbelieving attention, "that is a list of infractions against school rules. It tells me nothing about what you have done for him."

"Why should we do anything for him?" Bjelke asked. "There is a waiting list. His place at the school will be taken by noon tomorrow."

"Are you expelling the other boys?" Mor asked.

"All of them have perfect records, good marks. It is clear that-"

Mor interrupted again. This time, Bjelke's expression made Niels bet he thought Mor would be a discipline problem too, if she were Niels' age. Her tone was softer. "If you expel him, you reward this behavior. He wants to come home."

"Then find somewhere else to send him."

Mor laughed. "How do you propose I do that with an expulsion in his record?"

"We propose that you voluntarily withdraw him. Rinkobing has a nice selection of private and public day schools. Let him be home, let us maintain our impeccable reputation." Bjelke slid a single sheet of paper toward Mor. Niels craned his neck and verified that it was a withdrawal form.

She would sign it; he would be free to go home.

Bjelke passed her a pen and showed her where to sign. She tapped the pen three times against the paper before looking up at the headmaster. "You're certain there is nothing you can do?"

"The decision was unanimous," he said in an apologetic tone.

Mor sighed and signed the form. She set the pen at an angle across the page. "I'll ensure the boys are packed and out of their dorm by dinner," she said.

The defeat in her voice triggered an unexpected guilt in Niels. He hadn't thought about what this would do to her; only about being home, being together as a family.

"Boys?" Bjelke said. "You misunderstand: Eddie is welcome to stay."

Mor looked down at the withdrawal form

"Please," Eddie said in his softest voice. "I don't want to stay here without Niels."

Mor looked at Eddie and he nodded once.

She picked up the pen. "I'll need a second withdrawal form, please."

Bjelke looked at Eddie. "Don't give up your future over this. You have many friends here, opportunities you'll lose if you leave."

Eddie rested his folded hands on Bjelke's desk and explained in a calm tone, "I would like to devote more of my time to music."

"Do you think Dirigent Cattaneo's special interest in you will continue if you leave this school?" Bjerke asked. His skin was tinged with the faintest trace of red. Niels sat up with interest. All of Niels' antics had drawn a purple color from the headmaster. This redness...was it fear?

Eddie shook his head. "I don't know."

"It was my friendship with Cattaneo that earned you the chance to work with him; you should reconsider before giving that up."

"Excuse me," Mor said. "It was Eddie's talent that caught Giuseppe Cattaneo's interest. If the National Symphony Orchestra drops him, I am sure he will have no trouble finding other arrangements."

Bjelke pressed his hands together in front of his mouth, mimicking a prayer. He studied them with a thoughtful expression. "I'll speak to the directors," he said. "It's possible we can make other arrangements for Niels."

Eddie's fame could ruin this whole thing? *Months* of work, he'd put into getting out of this place, and Eddie's reputation would force him to stay.

Mor smiled at the headmaster, the warmest light in her eyes. "Thank you for helping us to understand your motivations." She squeezed Eddie's hand and he looked back at her with a smile on his face. "But you did say that Eddie participated in the theft of the school van. And...where did you find the liquor?"

Bjelke looked at the papers. "In Niels' dorm room."

"The boys share a room, do they not?" Mor asked.

Bjelke nodded.

"Then you can't be sure the liquor wasn't Eddie's. I think you'll have to recommend that he withdraw too, in order that he does not damage the school's impeccable reputation."

Bjelke frowned. "Let's not be rash. We may be able to put Niels on prob-"

Mor stood. "I'm afraid the decision is unanimous, Headmaster." She offered him her hand. "Thank you for taking the time to meet with us today. We'll expect a prorated tuition refund within thirty days."

After shaking Bjelke's hand, she walked to the door. "Let's go, everyone; if we hurry we can still set up a tree."

Two hours later all of them piled into the car.

"Would you like to drive?" Mor demanded frostily. "Since you have experience?"

"No," Niels held the front passenger door open for Eddie. No way would he sit up front with Mor this mad at him.

"Liquor?" Mor asked. "How often have you been drinking? And where in the *world* did you get liquor at your age?"

Niels sat in the backseat, squeezed between Viggo and the door. "Older students have it," he said. "It was easy to get; just-"

Eddie cut him off. "I did their homework for them."

"You?" Mor bit back her shock. "Please tell me you are covering for Niels."

"No," Eddie said. "And we never drank it except once to taste it."

Mor pulled out of the school parking lot, and in a moment they were on the eerily quiet streets of Copenhagen. If it weren't Jul, these roads would be busy, crowded, alive. "What did you need it for, if not to drink?"

"They might have been doing surgery," Cille suggested. "Or disinfecting wounds."

Niels laughed. "Or Bjelke might have hallucinated it."

Mor ignored Niels and glowered at Eddie, waiting.

"We sprinkled it on our clothes, our beds, our books..." Eddie looked at her. "We *wanted* to get caught and come home. We hate it there."

"And the riot?" Mor asked, turning down a side street. "What does he mean by that?"

"That wasn't on purpose," Niels defended. "It was a debate about whether we should have to wear uniforms, and by the time I was done half the class had stripped down to their smalls."

"Did you close your eyes during the debate?" Mor asked.

"What?"

"You said *by the time you were done*, which means you somehow failed to notice and stop talking before the situation got out of control. I'm trying to sort what caused that failure of common sense."

Niels couldn't decide whether to tell her the truth, that it was just a great speech and he got caught up in how awesome the whole thing felt, or shut her down and say the teacher hallucinated the whole thing. It wasn't like normal students would strip like that. A hallucination was far more likely.

"Going home isn't better," Viggo warned. They were in the BMW, which meant that in the back seat their shoulders were all squished together. Viggo's shoulders were hostile, stiff.

Eddie swiveled from the front seat. "It will be now. I promise."

"Maybe," Viggo shrugged. "There's no Julemanden. No presents."

No presents? Niels met Mor's eyes in the rearview mirror. What was *wrong* with her? Viggo needed distraction and fun, not a cloak of misery.

"Jul will be over tomorrow," Niels pointed out to Viggo.

He crossed his arms and made a *tuh* sound that felt too old for him. "And then you will never go to school again? Be no one?"

"We want to start a band," Eddie said.

Mor rolled her eyes.

She was so unfair. Ditching them at school on the biggest holiday of the year, rolling her eyes at their plans. Why shouldn't they be good at music? They'd been playing most of their lives, Eddie was arguably the most talented child musician in western Europe. Look what Niels had done to a class of bored students...imagine what he could do to an audience with music he loved.

"Without Far?" Viggo asked.

"No, we thought we'd include him," Niels snapped. He felt bad as soon as the words were out of his mouth. If Mor hadn't rolled her eyes, he wouldn't have been sarcastic with Viggo.

"You don't have to be mean to him just because *you* got in trouble," Cille told Niels hotly. She'd drawn a Jul tree in the condensation on her window.

Niels frowned at it, somehow even more surly. "He doesn't have to ask annoying questions just because he's little."

Viggo scrunched his legs up so his heels caught the edge of the seat, and leaned his head back against the middle seat, eyes closed.

"Why a hospital, of all places?" Mor asked.

If she wanted to roll her eyes, maybe she didn't deserve to know. Niels stared out the window at all the glowing, happy homes.

"So they could sing to dying people," Viggo answered.

Eddie whirled around and faced Viggo. "How did you know?"

"Because," Viggo said, with all the snark of a sixteen-year-old girl (Niels had met a few at school, girlfriends of the older boys), "We ran out of them."

"Fuck you!" Niels growled.

"Niels!" Mor slammed on the brakes in an intersection and glowered at him. When she started driving again, she decided, "We'll find you both another school."

"We'll just do the same thing," Niels warned. It would be great if they could avoid the middle part, where they got sent off to different schools over and over again until Mor finally let them stay home.

"I won't go back either," Viggo growled in Niels' same tone.

Mor sighed. "Back where, exactly, Viggo?"

Viggo crossed his arms. At his size, it looked more like he was hugging his seatbelt than like he was angry. "Back where you want me to go. Back home. If they get to be home, I want to go away."

Everything. They'd given up their whole futures at school so they could be there for Viggo, and he didn't want them?

"We're doing this for you," Niels told him.

"No," Viggo muttered. "You're doing it to sing and make dying people forget everything is broken."

No. This was about making *living* things forget everything was broken; living things named Viggo and Cille.

Mor pulled the car to the curb in front of their Copenhagen house. "You'll have to stay home until you're old enough to go away to school," Mor explained to Viggo. "If you still want to leave then, I'll help you select a school."

Viggo glared at Niels. Niels glowered back; where did Viggo get off whining about how much being home sucked, and then turn around and be pissed off at them when they tried to make it better?

"Have you been using our music equipment?" Niels accused. "Is that why you don't want us home?"

"No," Viggo said indignantly. He was *so* lying.

Niels looked at Mor. Fine, Viggo didn't want them at home. There was an easy solution: "Eddie and I could live here in town and go to day school," he suggested.

It would be great: No dorm rules, no Mor bossing them around, eating whatever they wanted.

Viggo climbed across Niels' lap and ran out of the car, into the house.

Mor frowned after him and rounded on Niels. "I hope you're happy," she said. She didn't sound like she hoped he was happy at all. If anything, he thought she hoped he was even more miserable than he was. She lifted the trunk open and said coldly, "Get your things inside and come help with the tree."

She stormed off and Cille trailed away after her. It was him, Eddie, and the falling snow.

"I'm sorry," Niels said. "I thought he would be happy."

Eddie grinned and passed a folded piece of paper to Niels. It was a contract for the Danish National Symphony Orchestra, inviting him to conduct ten shows at- "Three hundred *thousand* kroner per show?" Niels gaped at him. He did the math in his head. "We could buy our own house in under a year."

Eddie laughed at that ludicrous idea. "Or fund a band?"

It wouldn't make Viggo happy, though.

Niels lifted his school trunk out of the car and let it crash into the snow.

"I wanted to quit," Eddie told him in a quieter voice. "I can't do practices with the DNSO *and* do school. And Viggo and Cille and Mor are all miserable."

Niels looked at him. He'd never called Mor that before. They weren't just step-brothers, they were *brothers* and both of them cared about Cille and Viggo.

"Come on," Niels said. "Before the snow buries our trunks."

They dragged them up the walk and into the house together, letting them fall with a *thunk* in the entryway. The house was cold and silent. "Have you told her about the orchestra?" Niels asked.

Eddie shook his head. "She wants to be mad at us today."

It was better than her fake cheerfulness all the time. He'd take the anger, because it was real.

She came into the room, her hair down and her gloves off. "Viggo is gone," she said. She moved frenetically toward the door and then back into the house. "No, he went out the other way," she said under her breath.

Shit. Christ. Fuck everything.

Her terror was real too, but he wasn't as enthusiastic about that as the anger because Viggo...

Most of the row houses in Copenhagen surrounded courtyard gardens that were completely enclosed, but of course *their* row house did not. Their courtyard had an opening.

It was snowing; Viggo would be easy to track, slower at running than Niels.

"I'll get him," Niels said. He brushed past Mor, too angry to find any other words. If Niels had found Viggo gone, he would have left to chase him already, he wouldn't be in the house muttering to himself about what to do.

He ran past the front stairs, through the hall and the dining area, through the kitchen, and out into the courtyard. Sure enough, Viggo's fresh footprints marked the ground

He ran blindly in the cold, gloveless and coatless because he'd expected to go from the school to the car to the house without ever getting cold. His thin-soled athletic shoes slipped and slid against the snow-slick pavement as he ran, but he managed to only fall once.

He trailed Viggo down the narrow bricked Sofiegade and onto Overgaden and froze in place, eyes on the canal, struck with the sudden terror that Viggo might have jumped into the water. But no: His footprints went toward the Torvegade bridge, across the canal.

Maybe he'd gone to the church. Nope...he'd gone right off of Torvegade back onto the slippery bricks of the Overgaden that followed this side of the canal. *Where* could he go, on an island like this? He cut up Bådsmandsstræde and onto Strandgade.

When Niels reached the second bridge, over a branch of the canal, he stopped in the snow, doubled over at the knees. He had a stitch in his side. How the hell could Viggo run this far *this* fast, in this cold weather?

Viggo didn't go to school in the city the way Niels did, he didn't know his way around. Niels was taking too long to find him. It was cold, windy, not okay for a little kid to be out in.

Like Niels, Viggo didn't have a coat.

He took off again, over the bridge and through the neighborhood of newer apartment buildings.

Before he got to the bridge to the mainland, Viggo had veered off across a parking lot, toward a gazebo-like building along the canal, where people could rent canal tours of the city.

Inside the gazebo, Viggo sat against the wall shivering, while tears streamed down his face. Niels collapsed against him, almost crashing into him, as he smothered him in a hug that was half relief and half sobs. "Christ. You scared me, Viggo."

"Why do you want to come back?" Viggo asked, when Niels' breaths finally calmed down. "I have to be home and remember and everyone calls me his name and everyone at school tells me I'm going to die."

Niels hadn't thought of the name thing. He'd always envied Viggo having their far's name. When he was little, he'd even thought it meant Viggo was the one who would inherit their family estate, Falkhus. He knew better now, but he still had no idea why his parents had named Viggo after Far and given Niels a name that wasn't anywhere in family history.

It hadn't occurred to him that sharing Far's name would be agony now. That it might feel like replacing him, or never living up to him.

"Mor doesn't care," Viggo added. "She just says everything will be okay. *You* got to escape!"

No, he hadn't. He and Eddie had spent the fall and most of last spring surrounded by a bunch of rich snobs who insisted that because their fars were gay they must be too.

Niels knew — maybe too well for comfort — exactly what Viggo went through at school. "You think I don't know how bad it is? That's why we're coming home." He leaned his shoulder against Viggo's. "What about a nickname?"

He shook his head.

Niels got it; if he had Far's name it would be...what was the expression? A blessing and a curse. But he would never want to let it go.

Viggo tilted his head up toward the glass ceiling of the gazebo, eyes on the stars. "I think Cille is happy he died. She likes when things die."

Niels watched the stars too. It was easier than watching Viggo's face. "I think Cille is *relieved* he died, because it was so awful. She cries all the time. She calls me on the phone crying when Mor is in the garden."

He could see Viggo's surprise, but neither of them spoke for a while. Then Viggo announced, after a drawn-out breath, "Mor is going to die."

Given that two-thirds of their parents had already died, that was a reasonable fear. Niels nodded. "Everybody dies eventually." He hoped Mor would be healthy for a long time, decades, long enough for all of them to get adulty and boring.

Viggo kept his knees scrunched to his chest and did a little mini-walk that edged him in a semicircle so he faced Niels without ever standing up. He stood there, back hunched, and met Niels' eyes. "She takes the same medicine Far took. She hides it."

Oh shit.

Maybe he was wrong though. A lot of pills looked the same, maybe he was just...maybe.

No. Far had taken dozens of pills a day. Even if Mor took *different* pills, the fact that she took a bunch either meant she'd developed a love of vitamins since term started, or she was sick.

If she had the same thing, it meant Far had given it to her. It wasn't like other diseases that just happened to people, it was *done* to people. Edvard had gotten Far sick, and Far…

The gazebo blurred around him as Niels' vision clouded with tears of rage. It couldn't be. Far had loved Mor, he would never—

But Far loved Edvard too.

Niels stood. "Come on. Will you show me at home?"

Viggo nodded and took the hand Niels offered to help him up. They followed the canal back this time, ducking under a spiral staircase before crossed the bridge and wove their way to Sofiestrade. Walking was a lot easier than running, but it took ten times longer and Niels' fingertips were tingling by the time they stood in the courtyard behind their house.

"Will she give up, if we sing together?" Viggo asked.

Something in Niels melted. What was it like for Viggo to be so young and sing Far to his death?

He pulled Viggo against him. "Look at her. She's not even sick. Even if she has it, it could be years." Maybe even decades, like he hoped. He knew most people who got it lived a lot longer than Far and Edvard had.

If Mor died too, where would they go? What would happen to their home? Niels had no answers, only guesses, and they were the scariest part of all.

He and Viggo sneaked in through the kitchen and up the back staircase behind the enormous hearth. From deeper inside the house, they could hear muted voices; Niels bet Mor had called the Politiet to find them. The tree probably wasn't even set up yet, nevermind presents or food or any of that.

In Mor's bedroom on the second level, Viggo unzipped her flowered duffel bag and pulled out an entire zipper case full of pill bottles.

One of them he knew right away. It was a distinct indigo pill about the same size as the last joint on Niels' smallest finger. *Antiretroviral* was what Far had called it. There were the bright orange ones, the red and black ones, the little round pink ones...

Niels set the bottle down on the lace coverlet that decorated Mor's bed.

He wanted to sit, but if he left a print on the bed Mor would know he'd been in here. What they needed to do was go back outside and come in the front. They could get lectured by the Politiet about being careful and not running away.

He looked at Viggo. "This. *This* is why Eddie and I need to be home."

"Don't tell her you know," Viggo whispered. He returned the pill bag to the suitcase with painstaking care and sealed the bag, letting the zipper rest in the same spot as when they'd opened it.

"Eddie and I will make money," Niels promised. Thank Christ Eddie had a contract with the orchestra. "We'll make sure everything is okay, forever. We promise."

Viggo stuffed his hands in his pockets. "You can promise, but nothing will be okay."

No, the world was broken.

"I know," Niels breathed. He rested Viggo's head against his shoulder and hugged him forever against the truth.

6

SECRECY

It was a Jul of secrecy.

He should have known Mor would smell the klejner cooking in the kitchen; should have known she would investigate.

"Niels!" she gasped from the doorway. "What in the world do you think you're doing?"

"Making Jul," he said. He didn't meet her eyes. If she wanted to keep things from him and treat him like a little kid instead of an adult, then she didn't deserve to know any of his business. "The pudding is in the fridge, I already cooked the other food."

She walked along the counter and the stove and studied all the dishes set out on the enormous woodblock table in the center of the room. She stopped last at the pan of oil on the stove and turned it off. "If you spilled this, you could melt your skin off."

Niels stared at the plate of already-made klejner. "I didn't melt my skin off."

"But you *could* have. That is the point."

Technically, so could she. She wasn't a magically safer cook just because she was a female or because she was a mom.

He ate a klejner and debated his response: He could be evil and say the worst thing, that when he was only eight Far thought he was old enough and surely *six* years later he could handle it; he could be logical and point out that he'd already made a plate of klejner and *still* hadn't melted his skin off; or he could back down.

He moved the plate of treats to the table. Mor didn't need extra stress, even if she deserved it.

She frowned at him. "I want you to go to the cellar and think about the history of this house and this family. Think about what would happen if you burned it down."

He hesitated. She was right. If the house got damaged *and* she died, where would they live?

"I get it," he said. He looked toward the door. If he could get out of here, escape this lecture...

"I said *go*. The cellar. Now."

Christ, she was bossy. This was what he got for even trying to make a nice Jul for everyone.

"How long do I have to stay down there?" he asked. She'd never sent him to the cellar as a punishment before. It was a new low in an ongoing battle of wills between them.

The joke was on her; his music equipment was down there. He would just go play some dissonant chords loud enough for her to hear. Jace would be here soon for rehearsal and Jul dinner since his mor was in the hospital.

"As long as it takes," she said with a huff. She pointed toward the cellar door. "Now."

He made his way down the cellar steps at a painstaking pace, mostly to annoy Mor because he was certain she wouldn't do anything else until she'd seen him turn the corner at the landing.

He waited around the corner for a minute or two and then peeked back up the stairs toward the kitchen. Mor had stopped watching the stairs, but she was still in the kitchen. She ate one of the klejner, her eyes closed as she chewed it.

Good. She needed that more than he suspected she would ever admit.

He descended the rest of the stairs into the low-ceilinged stone cellar where most of his relatives were interred. Plumb lines hung from random areas of the ceiling, placed to measure changes to their house's foundation every so often.

He passed the racks of vintage and the shelf of liquors and beers no one had touched since Far died. This hallway of the cellar led him under the chapel, through the crypt. His grandparents, Giani and Cide, were interred down here, each with an engraved silver plate to mark their interment site. Then there was the empty tomb, that should have been Far's except Far had insisted on being cremated like Edvard.

Niels touched the stones outside the tomb and pretended Far *was* there. The day they'd thrown his ashes into the moat to be part of the land forever, Niels had seen Mor toss her ring into the blue-brown water as well. It had almost been two years since then.

When Niels had kids — *if* he had kids — Far's name would never be down here for them to know and ask about. He wouldn't be part of family lore in the same way.

He'd chosen cremation — a complete rejection of family custom — and Niels didn't know why.

He walked away from the empty tomb. Far had done a lot of things Niels didn't understand, and the older he got the less he understood them.

He moved away from the chapel and under the wing of the house that was farthest from Mor's personal study. This was the wing where Far and Edvard had set up the music equipment, the dehumidifiers to keep moisture out of the electronics, the soundproofing on the walls.

He picked up his guitar from the equipment cabinet in the hall and froze.

Someone was in the room, singing. He stepped closer, ears trained on the subtle sound. It was Viggo, playing bass and singing the Nissemand song from their childhood.

He *knew* Viggo was lying about using their equipment!

But.

It was the Nissemand song. Any other song would have pissed

him off, but this song of all songs...He lifted his guitar, placed his fingers on the fret, and joined in once Viggo started the second verse.

He stepped into the doorway so they could sing together, and Viggo dropped his bass in surprise. "Sorry!" He picked the bass up just so he could set it down again more gently.

Niels strode into the room and shut the padded soundproof door behind him. "Why are you sorry?"

"I touched your stuff and you saw."

Nice. He wasn't sorry he'd touched the stuff, he was sorry Niels saw. Niels laughed at him. "I've known since last Jul. You can't lie for shit." He picked up the bass and pressed it into Viggo's hand. "Jace is coming soon. We want you in the band; we need a bass."

They'd found Jace last April when they'd visited the hospital in Stauning to deliver snackable foods to the family pantries in the hospital and do a small classic rock concert for some of the patients. Jace's mor had some kind of glial cell deathmass in her brain and Jace didn't have a far. The result was that when Gemma Nygaard was in the hospital, Jace stayed over at Falkhus in one of the spare bedrooms.

Niels lifted his guitar: He wanted to test Viggo's skills before Jace and Eddie came down, a chance for the two of them — as brothers — to make music together, like they used to do with Far.

They played the Nissemand song again and had moved on to Far's death song when Jace walked in with Eddie. "He...j." His eyes trained on Viggo in surprise. "Glæd...elig...Jul."

He didn't want Jace to mess this up, now that Viggo was finally being open about music. He held up one finger. "Take every fuck you own and shut it up. Glædelig Jul to you too."

Eddie went and sat at the drums, joining in as Niels switched from Jul tunes to Queen's *Radio Gaga*. Jace, inexplicably, went back into the hall. He came into the room after a few seconds, leading a girl older than Niels, who had curly hair and a bass guitar slung across her back.

Niels stopped playing. "Maybe the fucks should talk," he suggested at Jace.

"This is Li," Jace said. He glanced at Viggo, then back at Niels. "She plays bass."

"I'm sorry," Niels told the girl. He was sorry, too. Something about her lips kept making him want to stare at them. And bands with girls got more gigs usually. "We're not looking for a bass player. That's cool though."

Viggo set his bass down. "Yeah you are."

Christ. No. He'd *finally* gotten Viggo to play with him, and now some stranger-girl would ruin everything just by existing. "Viggo!" Niels said. If it came down to random girl or Viggo, Viggo won. He needed Viggo to understand that.

Viggo didn't answer Niels. He looked at Eddie, more nervous than Niels had ever seen him, and sat down at the keyboard. He played the opening piano to Queen's *Bohemian Rhapsody*.

It sounded...heartfelt. Real.

"I wouldn't have to switch back and forth anymore," Eddie pointed out. Their songs usually either had drum or keyboard, never both, because Eddie wasn't two people.

Niels looked at Li. He tried to look somewhere besides her lips...her hands? Her bass? Anywhere but her face. "What can you play?" he asked her left hand. "What's your style?"

"You sure?" she asked VJ.

He nodded. "Ja. It's not as cool, but I'm better at piano."

Apparently, yeah, he was. Way better.

Li nodded. She gestured toward the piano, toward Viggo. "Bohemian Rhapsody? Lead me in."

Viggo restarted the song without the vocal intro. Li could actually sing high enough to hit the *galileo*s, so kudos to her for that, but Niels wanted to see if she could handle their *real* sound, so as soon as *Bohemian Rhapsody* was over he switched keys and played the opening to Tool's *Swamp Song*. Eddie picked up the drums, and sure enough...Li joined in on her bass and kept up.

Niels switched keys without warning in the middle of the song. He knew Viggo and Jace could keep up: Viggo, because it was a game

Far had played with them, testing to see if they noticed key changes; Jace, because he was used to playing with Niels.

Li took two measures to catch it and adjusted to match them. Pure talent and skill and the way her lips moved when she concentrated on playing...

When *Swamp Song* was over, Niels glanced between Jace and Eddie and Viggo.

Jace shook his head. "I brought her. My opinion doesn't count."

Ja. That was fair.

"She's good," Viggo offered. "Better than me."

Eddie ran his fingers over his adam's apple, something he did when he was thinking. "Let's try this," he said. "See if you can improvise." He started a basic drum beat, with more of a swing feel than a straight rock back beat.

Niels started to play something in B major to see how she handled so many sharps and unusual chords. Viggo joined on piano, Jace on second guitar.

Then Li came in, doing her own thing that merged perfectly with their sound. With a signal from Eddie, the whole band dropped out and Li did a really cool bass solo, switching from the major scale to the minor scale partway through.

When she finished, she looked at Niels.

"Can you stay for dinner?" he asked. "We were going to rehearse after, for the New Year's gig we have."

She grinned at Jace before she said to Niels, "Ja. I can."

"It was the assumption I gave her," Jace admitted.

Niels was dying to know how the conversation had gone: Jace, about the same age as Viggo, trying to recruit an older teenage girl. He wondered what charm he'd used to convince Li to come, what Li had thought of the whole thing.

"Where did you meet?" he asked.

"The hospital."

Oh, Christ; was Li from a dying family too?

"No one is sick on my end," Li said quickly. "My sister was sick years ago. We volunteer now."

"No one is sick here either," Niels lied. Even Eddie didn't know about Mor; that was Niels' secret with Viggo.

"So I'm in for a trial?" Li asked. She had a sheen of sweat on her forehead and upper lip, from playing.

"Do you get stage fright?" Niels asked, to be sure. He didn't want to get to the New Year's gig and have her panic and back out at the last minute."

"Not yet," she said.

He couldn't figure out whether that meant she'd never played before and maybe she would get stage fright, or she'd played a ton and never panicked or gotten sick.

"Trial then," he decided, to avoid the issue. He didn't want to ask an older *girl* about vomiting. He offered his hand to her. "I'm Niels. Welcome to Chainskull Death."

She shook his hand. Her lips quirked up in a suppressed smile. "Lisanne. Li."

"What about me?" Viggo asked. "Am I in too?"

Niels looked at his eager face, his hands still on the keyboard, his little kid legs that could barely reach the pedals.

Far would be so happy.

Niels was so happy, like a warmth that spread into him just by imagining a future where he and Viggo were part of a team.

He looked at Viggo. "Honestly it's about fucking time."

7

ALMOSTNESS

It was a Jul of almostness.

It started out well enough: The usual just-our-family awkwardness at dinner. Cille and Mor argued about whether Cille could go to school in Italy like she wanted. She'd found some Catholic school in the foothills outside of Florence — "Please Mor? I would be in the *heart* of Monster country!" — and Mor was refusing. She kept falling back on distance, but Niels knew Mor was sick.

She probably wanted the time with Cille around while she was still healthy enough to enjoy it.

They were still at it while Niels and Eddie and Viggo ate their Jul puddings in silence. *No*, Mor did not want to try Florentine food. *No*, she did not trust the Italian justice system—

"Mor!" Cille groaned. "Why would I get arrested?"

Mor frowned. "That's what that American girl thought before she was framed."

Cille put her head in her hands and groaned into her bowl. When she looked up again, she flipped her hair over her shoulder and met Mor's eyes. "I promise to never kill my roommate *or* know anyone who will get murdered in the future."

Mor laughed.

Niels was tempted to bury his head in his hands too. This was about to get ugly, if Mor was laughing in a sarcastic way. He was trapped there. No one had found the almond yet and no one could leave until it was found.

Oscar Birky, the guy who managed Falkhus for Mor and made sure the place didn't fall apart despite her lack of experience taking care of an ancient house, stepped into the room. His father, Victor, had managed the estate before him.

"Excuse me, Baronesse: A young man by the name of Dylan Fraser has asked to speak with your children."

Mor looked at Niels like this was his fault. "Who is he?"

Two nights ago, their band had opened for a big band from the US. They'd won a competition to get the spot and done the biggest concert of their lives. "He's the *Quoth the Crow* guy."

Cille jumped away from the table and ran toward the enormous windows that looked out onto the side lawn. Dylan wouldn't be visible from there...what was she doing?

Oh, nice: She used her reflection in the glass to tidy her hair and undo the two top buttons on her blouse. Mor watched her, a frown on her face.

"Let him in!" Viggo begged. He ran towards the door at the same time Dylan walked into the room, almost crashing into him. He cleared his throat. "Hey. Want to have dinner?"

"Hey, kid," Dylan said. He ruffled Viggo's hair like he owned him. "What are you, fourteen?"

Niels stiffened: *He* was fourteen. Viggo was still a little kid. But Dylan knew that; Dylan wanted to make Viggo feel cool and mature, which Niels guessed he was okay with for now.

"Almost," Viggo said eagerly. He ushered Dylan further into the room so Mor could frown at him more intensely.

The problem was that Dylan looked like an American rockstar: spiky, dyed red hair, eyeliner, tattoos, stubble, face piercings. These traits probably made him the most evil person Mor had met in years.

"I heard there was pudding," Dylan said to Mor. He wore an expression that fell somewhere between hopeful and ingratiating.

Mor met him with her best cold smile.

Viggo groaned.

"Hej," Niels said, before Mor alienated Dylan completely. "No restaurants open tonight?"

Dylan laughed. He sat in a chair more toward the middle of the table, away from where everyone else sat, and smoothed his collared shirt.

Niels knew he'd *tried* before he'd come here, because Dylan usually wore t-shirts with holes in them, ripped jeans, boots so worn the soles flopped against the ground a second before his feet hit. He couldn't believe Mor was being this rude, when Dylan had on slacks and a button-down shirt, he'd showered, he had on new-looking shoes.

Dylan cleared his throat and addressed Niels, mostly. "You guys did a good job opening this week. A great job, actually. I wanted to talk to you."

Viggo sat upright and tried to glower at Mor. His face was too little-kid still, so mostly he looked like he was pouting. "*Don't* mess this up," he warned her.

Mor served Dylan some Jul pudding. "I'm Giana. You know the others."

"This is Dylan Fraser," Viggo said even though Mor already knew that. "He's the coolest person you'll ever meet."

"Yes," Mor said. "I understood that to be the case." She glanced at Niels, at Eddie, her brow angled in unexpected worry.

Christ. Did she think that if the band got a good opportunity to do more performances, they would somehow take on Dylan's lifestyle?

"How hard would it be to get the rest of your band here tonight?" Dylan asked Niels.

Niels pulled his cell phone from his pocket and texted Jace and Li to get their asses to his house as soon as possible. He looked up at Dylan. "It's Christmas, so we're...they might be busy."

Dylan winced. "I know, but I have to be in Milan by tomorrow night, so it was now or never."

"Can I get you anything more substantial than pudding?" Mor offered while they waited.

Dylan surveyed the table. "Do you have any Akvavit?"

Niels strummed his fingers against the table, eyes on Mor. She tensed her shoulders, her gaze downcast as she left for the kitchen and the bottles of Akvavit in the cellar.

Cille gazed at Dylan the same way Mor used to look at Far, but without the subtlety. Niels bet if she'd known Dylan would be here, she would have put make-up on and had a massive fight with Mor about that instead of about Florentine boarding schools.

Now she twirled her hair around her finger. "So," she said. She said it louder, two more times, until she finally had Dylan's attention. As soon as he looked at her, she blushed and twirled her hair tighter. "Do you." She coughed and turned more red. "Have a girlfriend?"

Oh, Christ, was she serious?

Dylan ducked his head, but not before Niels caught a smile there. When Dylan looked up, his expression was more serious. "Boyfriend, actually. Sorry."

That was a blatant lie. Dylan had a boyfriend the way lots of boys at school had girlfriends: Their girlfriend was whoever was interested right that minute. What Niels thought Dylan really meant was *you're too young, kid*.

Which, if Niels thought about it, was a good thing. He wasn't used to thinking of Cille as a girl, but he realized she was getting older. She *was* a girl, not just the weird sister that didn't play music with them, not just the walking encyclopedia of serial killers.

A girl. Christ.

He was glad Dylan was into guys.

"I've been practicing," Viggo told Dylan. "I know piano isn't as cool as guitars, but I've been trying new things out to make it work. Setting the mood."

"Well," Dylan said. He had this way of nodding when he talked. He wiped his nose and Niels tensed; Dylan better not have brought a cold into the house. "You guys definitely set a mood. All three concerts."

Silence dominated. Dylan seemed like he wanted to say more, but the whole band wasn't here yet.

Eddie talked shop with Dylan: a descant idea he had for a guitar solo for one of Dylan's songs. They ended up ducked together, a sheet of scrawled-on tab paper in front of them as they worked out the details. Niels watched. Eddie kept tucking his pencil behind his ear while Dylan chewed on the other pencil. They'd talk for a minute and then write more.

"We should try that," Dylan concluded. He grinned at Niels. "I might have to steal Eddie."

Niels laughed, but...

Something. He, didn't know what, but something was off about Dylan — not in a dangerous way, but in a not-quite truthful way. Niels shook his head. It was dumb; Dylan was here to offer them some kind of gig, Niels needed to not ruin it over a misplaced gut feeling.

Out the window, car headlights shone in the darkness across the causeway. Their estate had an enormous car barn with a small gravel parking lot in front of it. From there, visitors had to cross the magnolia-lined causeway.

Viggo burst up from the table and ran into the foyer. A few seconds after he swung open the massive front door, a chill greeted them all in the dining room.

Mor came back finally, with the Akvavit, and poured Dylan a small serving of it before she set the bottle aside, up near her own seat. She called into the front hall, "Viggo! Please shut the door until Jace and Li are on the same side of the causeway as our house."

Niels ran his hands through his hair. Hopefully it didn't look flat and dumb like it sometimes did.

"Morrrrrr!" Viggo groaned from the hall. He slammed the door.

"You can't shut the door," Niels complained. "They'll think we don't want them here." Not Li's parents: They had an estate only a few miles away and their families had been friends in previous generations even if Mor hadn't been close to them before the band. "Especially Jace's mor. She thinks you're more important than you are."

If Mor had feathers, she would have ruffled them in response to that accusation. As it was, she could only straighten her back and smooth her skirt.

The door opened again a moment later; another rush of cold air in the dining room, followed by talking in the hall. Niels *knew* Viggo was whispering to Jace that Dylan was here throwing compliments around.

Everyone came into the dining room in a chaos of cold air and smiles and cheek-kisses. Mor brought food out for everyone, and after a few minutes they all sat around the table waiting for Dylan to talk.

He took a slow, thoughtful bite of food.

Viggo spoke up: "This is the best Jul since before Far died." He looked at Dylan. "He died on Jul."

Dylan cringed. "Ouch that sucks."

Another awkward silence.

Dylan looked at all the parents. "Thanks for coming, and I'm sorry for the bad notice. I didn't have a way to reach any of you except old-fashioned searches."

Everyone nodded.

"Did you need another opening act in Milan?" Viggo asked. All their hope was written on his face, in the wide set of his eyes and the way his mouth stayed half-open in a smile.

"No, that's booked." Dylan sniffled again.

Across the table, Jace deflated.

Niels' fingers tingled with weird energy. Not Milan, but Dylan was here. He wanted something.

Maybe something bigger than Milan.

Dylan addressed the parents again, more than the band. "I was actually looking for a more steady opening act for my US tour next spring."

Holy shit yes!

Now Dylan looked at the band. "Someone to travel with, someone to learn the ropes and be consistent instead of a new group at every stop."

"Yes," Li said. She had the most gorgeous smile that lit up her eyes brighter than a Jul tree. She hesitated and looked at Niels, at Eddie and Jace and Viggo. "I mean..."

It was a question.

Niels decided it was his job to answer. "Holy fuck. Are you serious?"

Every parent in the room frowned, except Jace's mor who laughed because she was awesome.

"Wait a moment," More argued. "They're all young. Children!"

"Children grow up!" Viggo begged. "This is an opportunity to be more than our ages, Mor."

She sighed. "Adulthood lasts fifty or sixty years, if you're lucky." She was shaking her head. Somehow, impossibly, she intended to refuse Dylan.

Niels' fingers curled into fists under the table.

"Childhood is only twenty years," Mor finished. She'd made up her mind.

"We could all die any day," Viggo pointed out.

He and Mor had a staring match.

Niels glanced at Li, to see she was still smiling an enormously happy smile that made him wish he was the one who had made her feel that way, not Dylan.

Dylan was closer to her in age, in maturity.

Niels fixed his hair again.

Mor set her spoon down across her bowl. "From what I understand, dying any day is far more likely in the US than here. Look at Detroit. Chicago!"

"Grunge and Punk are more popular in the Pacific Northwest," Dylan told her. "Those cities have very low crime rates."

Mor frowned.

"You're dying here!" Viggo belted out. "What's the difference?"

Mor gasped. "I'm what?"

Niels couldn't look at anyone. Viggo had crossed a hard line, one they couldn't un-cross.

He pulled his hands down his face, stretching the skin.

"I don't know," Viggo said in a small voice.

"Mor?" Cille asked. Niels could tell from her pitchiness that she was crying.

Mor's answer to Viggo was stern. "My life is not *that* dull, that I feel like I'm dying, Viggo Poulsen."

It wasn't just stern: It was cold, layered with suppressed alarm.

"You're going to die," Viggo said instead of letting it go like a sane person. "Just like Far and Edvard. You have the same thing."

Cille was sobbing now.

"Where did you hear that?" Mor demanded with a chill she usually reserved for Niels. "No. I don't want to know. I'm tired of the rumors that circulate about this family."

Niels still hadn't looked up, but now he did: He caught Viggo's eyes and silently begged him to stop before he completely ruined everything.

"Your pill bottles learned to sing," Viggo insisted. "Are they rumors?"

Viggo and Mor had a staring contest.

Finally, Mor folded her hands across the table, her cheeks tinged in an uncharacteristic pink. "We'll discuss this later."

Viggo crossed his arms. "I want to go to America. It's *one* tour. Like..." He looked at Dylan. "Six months?"

Dylan sniffled again. "Maybe not even that long."

Mor huffed. "Who do you expect to be your guardians? You can't waltz off to America alone!"

"You could go with," Cille offered. "I could go to that school in Florence."

She got a dreamy look in her eyes that made her infatuation with Dylan look like a passing thing.

Jace set his spoon down; it was loud enough to draw everyone's attention. "My mor wil. She had to go anyway."

All the adults looked at Jace's mor, Gemma, who ducked her head and curled her hair behind her ear. That lock of hair was shaped like she kept it behind her ear constantly. "I know it's not traditional. Their medical system isn't as good as ours, but they have a doctor there who specializes in a new treatment for my cancer."

Mor opened her mouth. Niels *knew* she was about to ask who would watch the 'kids' if Gemma was in the hospital for a complication.

"Li's almost an adult. And she's old enough to babysit." Ouch. Did he really just say that? He looked at Jace, because Jace wasn't Li. He needed to change the subject away from the word *babysit*. Fast. "You knew about the US thing?"

Jace shrugged. "I knew she was going. I wasn't sure what I would do."

Stay with them, probably. Mor would have taken him in a heart-beat. Or Li's parents would have adopted him to pass on their family title..

"Great," Dylan said. "Glad that's settled." He reached into his grungy gray backpack and pulled out a stack of black and silver t-shirts. He passed one to everyone in the band and held the last one up to show a list of tour dates and cities printed on the back of the shirts. "I work out of New York, so I suggest getting settled there at least a month before the March concert."

Holy shit. A month before the first March concert was barely a month from now.

Gemma took the last shirt from Dylan. "That will work well. I can schedule my treatments around the concerts."

"What about money?" Mor asked.

Li's far sighed. "We'll provide a million toward the campaign," he offered. He didn't specify US Dollars or Krone or Euros. He talked to Li more than the rest of them: This was an investment in *her*, not in the rest of the band. "Six months, one million, and if you don't take off..."

Li nodded. She kissed each of her parents' cheeks, tears in her eyes. "Jeg elsker dig."

When she sat again, Mor explained, "I meant, who will pay them to do the concerts."

Li's far looked at Dylan, a challenge in his eyes. "That's Mr. Fraser's responsibility. They're fronting for the events, not booking their own."

Dylan laughed. "I mean...some of these venues only pay openers a hundred bucks. It's an opportunity for you to gain a fanbase, not make money."

Eddie shifted. He'd been so quiet that Niels almost forgot he was there. "We're already a big name," he countered. What he meant was that *he* was a big name; he'd already done a tour in the US as a guest conductor with Mor as his guardian, while Niels and Cille and Viggo were under the care of Oscar Birky at Falkhus. "With us you know you're getting quality. And unique. That's worth more than a generic opening band."

Dylan studied Eddie. "Two thousand," he offered.

"Five."

"Thirty-five hundred."

Eddie nodded.

Niels did the math quickly in his head. If they did three shows a month, that would be ten grand in US Dollars. Split between the five of them, it was only two, and after taxes it would be even less, but...they were doing it: They were showing Mor they would be okay on their own, have an income, be able to support Cille if they had to. And they would be doing a *lot* more than three shows a month.

"Three to six songs per show," Dylan insisted. "At minimum. No cancellations. No being too sick to play." He looked at Niels. "And you. Take care of your voice. I don't want to hear that you can't sing because you did something stupid."

Niels nodded. "Deal."

It didn't really sink in yet. Li and Jace shared a huge grin; Viggo smothered Mor in a bear hug. Eddie started eating again.

Cille burst into tears. Again. "I'll be stuck alone here with Mor? Because I'm a *girl*?"

No. She would be stuck here with Mor because she'd never played music with them, even when they all but begged her to on holidays.

"She's not really dying," Viggo said quickly. "She might die, but...she's not that sick."

"Yes she is!" Cille lashed out without warning and kicked Viggo squarely between the legs.

Hard. She was a vicious monster when she wanted to be.

"Hey!" Viggo groaned, doubled over at the waist. "I have research I can show you! I've been giving her the right snacks. She'll be okay."

Mor mouthed the words *right snacks?* under her breath. She told Cille, "I have what Far had that first Christmas Edvard and Eddie moved in. It has never progressed, and no one expects it to in the near future. Do you remember how healthy he was then?"

Cille nodded, silent.

Far had been healthy then, ja. And two years later he'd died.

"This is a lovely tablecloth," Li's mor said out of the blue. "Has it been in your family long?"

"It was my mother's," Mor said. "She got it in Hungary of all places."

No one said a word for the longest time.

Then Cille, crying more quietly now, whispered, "Far killed you." Her cheeks red and tear-stained, she glanced at Dylan with a heated expression. "I'm *never* getting married!"

"I'll marry you, Cille," Jace offered.

Cille's arm twitched like she might punch him.

He flinched. "And death shall we part immediately," he joked. He fluffed his hair and asked Dylan, "So when do we go?"

"By mid-February at the latest, you should be practicing at our studio. They may offer you an album too, with a contract."

"That's barely a month away," Niels said. He couldn't *believe* it! In a month, they would move to Manhattan! No more boring Danish countryside, no more arguing with Mor's rules, no more scrambling to find gigs close enough that Mor would let them go.

He needed to clear the dishes and pack his shit and throw a giant happy-scream party for himself in his bedroom where no one would hear.

New York! The City that Never Sleeps! Home of celebrities and skyscrapers and almost every culture in the world, all squeezed into a few hundred square miles.

Niels could practically taste the metallic flavor of traffic and smog and the throng of people all doing their own thing.

In the kitchen, hands full of dishes, he was surprised to see that Li had followed him. She wore a midnight blue dress that glimmered in the light. The butterfly sleeves moved when she moved, brushing against the pale skin of her upper arm.

She carried dishes too.

"We'll be famous!" he said. It was all he could think of besides her arms and he didn't want to think of those at all.

That huge smile came back to her face, her eyebrows up in twin happy, graceful arcs. "We're going to America."

She turned and leaned against the counter.

A dish sat on the counter behind her. He couldn't figure out how to get it without touching her. He stepped closer. Instead of reaching for the dish, his hands found her waist. They rested there, clumsy and lost.

He caught her eyes.

Just once. Just *once*, he wanted to know...

He stepped closer, without giving her the chance to panic and back away, and kissed her. The kiss was at least as clumsy as his hands on her waist.

When their lips met, her hands pressed into his back. They wanted *more*, not less.

He kissed her for real this time; hungry and hopeful and filled with an anguish he had not known existed. He slid his hands under her ruffled butterfly sleeves and onto the bare flesh of her back, drinking in her taste and her scent as he grazed her skin.

Her hands found their way down his back, into the waistline of his pants. A shiver coursed through his body as she slid her hands around to the front, against the skin between his hips.

He moaned into her mouth. He'd always known kissing her would be amazing, but this was beyond anything he had imagined.

This was the reason people wrote romance music, because of this feeling.

Something clanked behind them. Niels jumped away from her, guilty, ready to face Mor.

But it wasn't Mor: It was Viggo, his mouth open in surprise. "You'll ruin the whole band!" He warned. "You can't date! That's what destroys bands!"

And, according to Cille, lives.

He could still feel the heat of Li's lips and hands on him.

"You didn't see anything," Niels told Viggo.

"This is my only chance," Viggo told him, full of sudden anger. His voice cracked. "If you break up..." He slammed the dishes on the counter and left the room.

Shit. Christ. Fuck everything.

Li straightened her dress. "So." She started stacking dishes in the sink, sorted by size so they made a tidy pile for Niels to wash after everyone went home. "He's right. We can't date." Her eyes were on the dishes.

Niels just watched her work. His hands shook and he didn't trust himself not to drop any dishes. "Okay. Ja."

She met his eyes and her tension melted. "We could...one more kiss, and that's it."

"Or we could date and not tell anyone?" he suggested.

He could see their future together so well: stolen kisses, shared jokes, an intimacy of souls more than of bodies. Not that he would ignore the body part, he had plans for that too...

She studied him, hands against the counter behind her. "I want this too. The band. I don't have an estate waiting for me."

By Danish law, Li couldn't inherit the family title. If she had a son before her far died, her son could inherit, but otherwise...

Niels had an estate waiting, though.

He skimmed his fingers over the exposed skin of her upper arm. "You could."

Wait what? Had he just *proposed*?

Ja, he had. He realized he meant it, too. He could *see* their future together, hadn't he just thought that? The band stuff was temporary. When it ended, they would come home to Denmark and run the estate together and maybe have kids someday and he would *never* hurt her like Far had hurt Mor.

Li kissed him again; this time her hands found his waistline much faster and she skimmed her fingers along his skin with a more desperate desire he mirrored with his own frenetic touch.

She pulled away. "I want the band. I'm not interested in estates. I'm sorry."

She meant it, too; her tears said more than her words.

But she didn't want it. *Them*. Him. She didn't.

He tried to breathe. "It's fine. Really. I want the band too. I'm...I shouldn't have pushed that. I'm sorry."

"I wanted it," she promised. She reached for his hand and held it between hers. "I love you, Niels. If we ever retire, it's a yes. I'll marry you, I'll run the estate with you."

If.

He reminded himself that Mor needed him to have an income *now*, not when he was an adult. What if she got worse rapidly, without warning?

"If we make it that long single," he said, and he made it sound like a joke because the alternative, the question there, the knowledge that she was beautiful and about to be famous and would be married to someone more mature and more *everything* than Niels would ever be...that was too unbearable to address. The joke was easier.

"Even if we don't," she promised. She bumped into him and smiled. "We're going to be famous."

He tried to summon the thrill he'd felt only moments before. America. Fame. Money. Dating *might* destroy the band; it wasn't worth the risk when income and stability mattered more.

The other opportunity — a future with Li — slipped away like a song he only knew the opening riff of.

8

TERROR

It was a Christmas of terror.

It should have been fun: their first Christmas in America. Christmas lights were everywhere. Toys and wreaths and bows filled stores, lined streets, populated parades.

By now they knew this wouldn't be their only Christmas here. This would be home for years, maybe even decades.

Tonight's show was over. Who would have ever thought they'd be doing a concert *in* America *on* Christmas? Nothing energized him like being onstage in front of the kind of crowds *Quoth the Crow* drew, and according to the label they'd signed under, more and more people were starting to come to the concerts for *them*, not for Dylan's band.

Tonight's opening act had been ten songs before Dylan came onstage. Lately every time they did a show the managers added songs to their set.

Niels was alone in one of the backstage rooms, looking for where he'd set the extra guitar strings. He wanted to fix his guitar so he could find Viggo and Eddie and play the Nissemand song once before Christmas was officially over.

In the chaos of America, of touring and album-making and

learning new customs, he felt farther than ever from Far. He didn't want to give up the Nissemand song on Christmas; it felt like if he missed even one year, he would never do it again.

While Niels fished through the equipment bags in search of guitar strings, the door to the room opened and clicked shut. Twice — it clicked shut twice, like the door had been locked.

Niels looked up: Dylan was here. He looked at Niels with an intensity he'd never shown before. He was inexplicably *off*, not himself — his mannerisms askew and his expressions wrong for his face. It was like someone else was wearing his skin. Was he high?

"Hej," Niels greeted, wary. "Have you seen the strings?"

Dylan crossed to the mini fridge and got himself a beer. "You know, you used to tell me what a great concert I'd done. All of you, a whole band of ass-kissers. Now you just want to know where the guitar strings are." He popped the lid off the beer with his bare thumb and chugged half the bottle in one swallow. "They're *my* guitar strings. Buy your own."

"Sure," Niels said.

Dylan never really got angry — sometimes (once) he got scary calm instead of mad, but he'd never had a visible temper toward any of the band before. He'd never expressed jealousy, either..

Niels backed away, eyes on the door. Dylan *had* locked it.

"You know what?" Dylan said. "Take it. Take all the guitar strings. Take the rest of my fans. And then take your massive fucking ego and get the fuck out of my life."

"I'm good," Niels told him. "You're right; we should buy our own equipment and not use yours." He edged closer to the door. Dylan shifted closer to Niels.

"You're not leaving, are you?" Dylan challenged.

"Well..." This was a dumb idea, but it wasn't as much an idea as the words were already halfway out of his mouth. "You told me to get the fuck out of your life. I can't do that if I don't leave."

"Not yet," Dylan growled. "You owe me."

Niels waited to find out what Dylan thought he owed.

Dylan finished off the beer. He held the glass by its neck in his right hand, raised enough that Niels flinched even though Dylan was too far away to hit him and too out of it to aim with any accuracy if he threw it.

Dylan deflated and lowered the bottle. "You should have a beer with me. Before you go."

He got two more out of the mini fridge. Niels should have tried to leave, he knew that as soon as Dylan turned back around with the beers in his hand, but he was too frozen in some kind of weird fascination. He was scared, yes, but a sick part of his brain was curious what Dylan would do next.

There was also the fact that if he left, he didn't know if he would have a job anymore. He didn't want to ruin things for the whole band, just because Dylan scared the piss out of him.

Dylan opened both beers and sat down on the folding futon. He patted the seat beside him and held a beer toward Niels. "Sit. Drink."

Niels sat. He took the beer.

"Sip it," Dylan ordered.

Christ, this was bizarre. Niels took a drink. He liked the fizz, the way it almost masked the gross flavor, but he hated the aftertaste of whatever this shit was.

"Wrap your lips around the bottle when you drink," Dylan said.

Niels shook his head. "I'm not doing that." It was the kind of hazing ritual Niels would have expected when he was at boarding school. Not here, alone with a scary high guy who weighed at least fifty pounds more than Niels.

Dylan reached out, faster than Niels expected because of how out of it he was, and grabbed the loose flop of hair on the top of Niels' head, the one he flipped out of the way during concerts and somehow it made the crowds scream.

Now it made *him* scream — in surprise more than pain.

Dylan forced his head back and poured beer into his mouth while it was still open. Niels slammed his mouth shut and dropped his beer, grabbing Dylan's hands and pushing them away.

Dylan flipped him back further, releasing the upright part of the futon so it fell backwards behind them. He shoved Niels onto it and pinned him, knee on his chest and hands pinning Niels' hands against the pleather headrest.

Niels kicked, but Dylan's body was out of reach. He bucked, arching his back, but Dylan shifted so almost all of his weight was on that one knee. Niels couldn't breathe. He could feel his face changing colors while Dylan's knee pushed into his upper abdomen.

"You like Li?" Dylan asked, unexpectedly.

Niels didn't answer because he couldn't. His mind spun: What did Li have to do with pinning him down like this? Was Dylan going to kill him?

"I get to fuck one of you before I go home tonight. I'm taking my reward for finding your band, making you famous." Dylan said. "You can make this good, or you can go home and I'll find Li and let *her* make it good."

Shit. Was this who Dylan really was underneath his persona?

"Help!" Niels bellowed with the last of his breath, louder than he'd ever yelled anything in his life. He was scared, so the word came out too high to carry well. He tried to yell again, lower, but Dylan clamped his hand down over Niels' mouth. He was out of air anyway; Dylan intended to kill him.

Niels squirmed; he managed to free one hand, now that Dylan had shifted his weight. He pushed against Dylan's face with his free hand, clawing at it, desperate for air.

An explosion of noise startled both of them. Dylan jumped away from Niels.

All he could do was lie there on the futon, gasping for breath. There was a thump and a sobbing noise. Someone — a strange deep voice Niels almost recognized — growled low, "Stay away from him."

The sobbing got louder, and then there were footsteps running out of the room as the sobs faded.

Niels let out a long shaky breath. He was okay; alive, safe.

A human pyramid appeared in front of Niels' vision. "Are you okay?" it asked.

"Yeah," Niels said. His voice came out normal, despite everything. He sounded okay, so he must be okay.

The pyramid helped him up to a sitting position, folded the back of the futon up so it supported Niels' back again.

"Can I get you some water?" the pyramid asked.

Water. Ja, he needed a drink. His throat burned from not being able to breathe.

"Li," he said. "He's going to hurt Li."

"He won't," the pyramid promised. He tapped his earwig and mic. "I already warned people to make sure everyone else is safe." He offered his hand. "I'm John Dempsey, but everyone calls me Griff."

Griff.

Niels shook his hand. "Niels."

An odd, confused expression washed over Griff's face and then vanished, tto be replaced by something professional and efficient. Griff got him some bottled water from the minifridge and sat next to him on the futon.

"Are you really okay?" Griff asked while Niels drank the whole bottle in one long rush.

Niels shook his head when he finished. "No," he admitted. To his horror, he started to sob so hard it shook his whole body. Griff hugged him against him and rubbed his back. He made gentle promises, like that Niels was safe now and Griff wouldn't let Dylan hurt anyone in the band.

When Niels' breathing evened, he looked at Griff. The enormous man had been alert to trouble, broken down a door Niels was pretty sure was locked, saved him, scared the shit out of Dylan, gotten protection for the rest of the band, supported Niels when he cried the hardest he'd cried since Far died...

"Do you work here?" Niels asked.

"I do freelance security," Griff said. "Your manager hired me for this show and the New Years' one."

So he was local to New York. Better and better.

"Can I hire you?" Niels asked. He had no idea if he could even afford to pay someone's salary; he just knew he wanted the security. "Full time."

Griff reached into his back pocket and took a business card out of his wallet. "Call me in the morning and we can talk," he offered. "I think one of your band friends is on her way."

He must have gotten it through the earwig.

Niels used the hem of his shirt to wipe his face dry and nodded. He stood up, moved away from Griff so Li wouldn't suspect anything.

He tried to smile when she came in but he realized right away — from the way her eyes got wide and her mouth opened in an 'o' of shock — that it hadn't worked.

"Whoa," she commented. "Hej. What's going on?"

Griff nodded toward Niels. "You have my card." He left through the kicked-out door. Someone would have to pay for that. Niels bet it wouldn't be Dylan. A headache blossomed over his right temple, either from not being able to breathe or from having to replace the door.

He looked up. No, the headache was about Li seeing him now, like this. "Hej," he stammered. They'd done a concert. He should still be feeling good from it like he usually did. "That was fun. The concert."

What did he usually do after a concert? He couldn't remember.

Li hugged him. They hadn't hugged more than casual quick friendly hugs since the kiss last Jul. She still smelled the same, like home and like her shampoo and something soft and feminine under it that he couldn't identify.

"Hej," she said, soothing. She kneaded her fingers into the tight muscles of his back.

"I don't want to tour with them anymore," Niels admitted. He would always be scared, worried Dylan would find a way to be alone with Li.

Li stepped away so she could see his face, study him. "What happened?"

He didn't want her to be scared. Griff would keep her safe. They would get away from Dylan. Maybe Niels would get lucky and never have to see him again. "I just think we're doing well enough on our own."

He hated lying to Li, of all people. They needed to get away from Dylan, and Li would never have to know.

She nodded. "We can go alone."

"Are you okay?" he checked.

"No." She sighed. "Ja. But something happened to you."

"Something *almost* happened," he promised. "It didn't happen." He would never shake that feeling — the realization that Dylan could have done anything to him: rape, murder, who knew what else. Niels was powerless, vulnerable...

He looked at Li. "You're a girl."

She laughed. "Ja?"

"Do you feel..." Was this how all men made people feel? Helpless and weak? Did Far make Mor feel this way?

Last year, when he'd kissed Li...was this why she'd stepped away from him, refused to date him?

"Like prey?" he finished.

Her expression hardened. "Did Dylan...?"

"That guard guy showed up. So no." That was all Niels wanted to say about any of this. He never wanted her to know Dylan had threatened her.

"Sometimes," she said. "Not around the band, but." She shrugged. "Sometimes."

It took him a minute to realize she was answering his question about feeling like prey.

Fuck Dylan. Except not literally. "I think I might hire that guard full time."

"Do it," she said. She was firm, decisive.

"For all of us, not just for me. And when someone makes you feel uncomfortable, you can just..." he wanted her to feel safe all the time. He needed it, more than he needed himself to feel safe.

She opened her mouth and almost said something. Then she tried again. "I said yes to Dylan. He hasn't hurt me."

She'd been with Dylan. She didn't want Niels, but she'd slept with

Dylan Petri Dish Fraser. He struggled to find words, but finally managed, “You’ve slept with him?”

She looked away. “Ja. Not exclusive. He doesn’t do exclusive.”

She wouldn’t even *kiss* Niels again, but she would sleep with Dylan? He didn’t understand. Something was wrong with him, something deep and integral, something that made Dylan think he could control him and made Li not want him at all.

She would rather be with someone who didn’t even treat her with respect, than with Niels. Someone who slept around, someone who probably carried-

The panic hit him like a tsunami. “Li be *careful*. Look what happened to my fars!”

What if she got sick? What if she was already sick?

“I’m not touching him again,” she said. Her voice was strange, flat, miserable. “Not after this.”

It might already be too late though. Dylan could have gotten her permanently sick.

His hands shook now for an entirely different reason.

“Do you love him?” he breathed.

She laughed for some reason. “No. I love you.” She cleared her throat. “I love this band. I don’t love Dylan. It was all favors.”

“Favors?” Why couldn’t she just love him for *him* and not for the band?

No. That was such a babyish thing. They were successful, gaining traction, selling more copies of their first ever album every day.

She shrugged, suddenly interested in the poster over the minifridge. “He helps us, w- I help him.”

We. She’d almost said we. He let it go; he decided he didn’t want to know who the other one was, whoever else was sleeping with Dylan. He didn’t want to know if she was sleeping with that person either, if *no dating in the band* really meant *I don’t want you*.

What mattered was that she thought she had to sleep with Dylan to keep the band safe.

He’d thought almost the same thing, but unlike Li he’d fought and maybe almost died.

Li did it for them, for all of them. She shouldn't ever have thought she needed to do that. "Is that good for you?" he asked, because maybe she liked it and *for the band* was an excuse the same way *no dating in the band* was.

"Does it matter?" she snapped. She took a deep breath and relaxed her tone. "This isn't a lifestyle for dating."

Ja, he'd gotten the message loud and clear.

He didn't want to make her feel like prey, anyway. He didn't want to make *anyone* feel that way, ever. He could just be the weird single guy forever and never catch any STDs or hurt anyone.

He needed a change, a token to remind himself to stay away from Li. "I think I want to bleach my hair."

It wasn't just about staying away from Li, it was about...

Dylan. Niels wanted to look tougher so guys like Dylan would get the message and stay away.

Li flopped back on the futon, right where Niels had been before Dylan pushed him over. "Ja?"

"You think it will look good?" Scratch that: He didn't want to know if she thought it would look good.

She laughed, alight with amusement. "It will look horrible. Can I help?"

Trust someone who didn't want to be with him, to help him look as bad as possible. "I'll look more Danish."

She thought for a second. "You're cutting my hair," she decided. "I'm dying yours."

She wanted to *cut* her hair?

He refused to be responsible for that travesty, when her parents found out and looked for someone to blame. "Isn't your hair a Danish national treasure?"

"I'll mail it home."

He laughed, too hard, because he knew she would follow through and mail it, and her parents would open a baffling package with nothing but her hair, probably in a neat braid so it all stayed together.

They went to the drugstore for some dye and makeup and a hair trimming kit. They took the subway home and did each other's hair.

It didn't occur to him until almost dawn that he'd never found Viggo and Eddie, never sung the Nissemand song.

When he realized it, something inside him hardened in a permanent way. Li, Far, romance: He was done being sentimental about things he couldn't have.

9

DREAD

It was a Christmas of dread.

Niels thought for sure by now, if Viggo was coming back he would be back. At this point, Niels doubted he would be found alive.

He'd lost Viggo. Failed him. He didn't even want to think about what could have happened to him. He didn't want to, bit he couldn't turn off his mind...kidnapped, raped, mugged and left for dead, thrown in the river...

Shutting the thoughts down was impossible.

He sat next to Eddie on the couch, both of them in an adrenaline hangover.

"I keep replaying it in my mind," Eddie said. "He was right there in the hall. What if one of us had stayed with him?"

"Fuck if I know," Niels muttered. He had a headache across his forehead and a soul ache across his heart, to match. Viggo...

One of the officers sat in a canvas fold-out chair, facing Niels and Eddie. "Since you can't stop replaying it, do you mind running through it again for us?"

Eddie opened his mouth, probably to say something nicer than what Niels was thinking (How about you assholes do something useful like run through the security footage again?). The problem was the security footage. It was baffling: The band milled in the hall outside the recording area, then they went in the room. Viggo dropped his wallet, stopped to pick it up, and...vanished. Poof, gone.

The cops said someone had tampered with the tapes. That made it sound deliberate, coordinated. If it was a crime of chance, it would have been on camera.

There was only one person affiliated with the studio who Niels thought might have hurt Viggo: Dylan Fraser. He had a solid alibi supposedly.

Eddie opened his mouth but Niels didn't hang around to hear what he said: They'd been over this all so many times. Instead he went down the hall to look in Viggo's room again. Maybe there was something — anything — Niels hadn't noticed before...a phone number, a calendar...Niels would take anything at this point.

He opened the door and froze on the threshold.

Viggo lay in the bed, shoulders hunched and shaking like silent sobs wracked his body. He was *here*. How? That wasn't even possible. They'd checked his room over and over, the cops had gone through his shit, there was no way he'd gotten in the apartment door without anyone noticing.

"How the hell did you get in here?" Niels asked. A sob burst out of somewhere and he ended up sitting on the edge of Viggo's bed, Viggo tangled in his arms. Both of them cried for a few minutes.

Viggo wiped his eyes eventually and shifted away from Niels. "I can't tell you how."

How what?

Oh. Ja. How he got in here.

Niels nodded toward Viggo's bedroom window, hundreds of feet above the ground. "Well you didn't get in that way, and you didn't get in through the door."

Viggo's eyes, weirdly hollow behind the redness from crying, widened. "Magic. I was abducted and taken to this place and..." He held his hand out toward Niels: In it was a tea bag without the little string and paper tag. "I only have one."

Actually Niels had a whole tin of those out in the kitchen, because even with her child missing Mor took time to drink tea.

Either way, it definitely wasn't magic. "Viggo, that's a tea bag."

"No it's not!" Viggo's voice cracked. He gripped Niels' wrist, a determined expression on his face, and-

Suddenly they were somewhere else, except that wasn't possible. It must be a hallucination.

Niels had a fraction of a second to take in the world's girliest pink froofy bedroom before a blonde girl an inch or so taller than Viggo said, "You came back?"

On the bed, a giant white cat — was that a fucking *snow leopard*? — twitched its tail and said, "Of course he did. I told you."

Talking cats. Definitely a hallucination.

"My brother," Viggo said. He had this look on his face, like Laney was the sun and he was the moon and Laney was the only thing that gave him light. He turned to look at Niels. "See?"

Ja, Niels saw: Viggo's hands must have some kind of drug residue on them and now Niels was hallucinating.

Except. Did people *know* when they hallucinated? If this was what being high was like, it was way overrated.

"Usually," the blonde girl scoffed affectionately, "when you run away you don't come back. I think it's a rule to running away. Like a guideline: Steal money, don't go back." She tilted her head. "You didn't steal any money either."

"Laney!" VJ crossed the room to where the girl sat at a wooden vanity. "I ran away for five minutes. Some people call that a bathroom break."

"I *took* a bathroom break, and you were gone when I got back." She pushed some of the vanity drawers closed. She met Viggo's eyes in the mirror. "Stay this time?"

"No," Niels said. Maybe if he pushed back the hallucination would take the hint and go away.

"We're not even married yet and you're nagging me," Viggo complained, like Niels hadn't said a word.

"Yet?" Niels breathed.

He tried not to panic or look at the talking snow leopard in case looking at it validated its existence. He breathed. In, out, nice and slow. He could smell the room, the hot late-morning sunlight, even some kind of girly perfume.

Did hallucinations have smells?

"We're betrothed," Viggo explained, like *that* was normal at his age. "This is another realm. I was..." He cringed. "I got in some trouble and she saved me." He nodded toward the cat, not Laney, when he said who saved him.

"Some trouble?" How much trouble could he even get in at the studio?

Viggo blushed and looked away. "Yeah."

Oh, shit. Niels was right about Dylan.

Or this was a hallucination and fake-Viggo was telling Niels exactly what he expected to hear.

"Dylan?" Niels asked, to confirm before he went and kicked Dylan's ass when he got home.

Viggo shook his head.

If it was a hallucination, wouldn't he have told Niels what he wanted to hear?

"Did..." Viggo searched Niels' face. "...he do something to you?"

"It's Laney, actually," Laney interrupted. "Not Dylan; that's a boy's name."

"Dylan is a band guy," Viggo told her in a tender voice. He turned back to Niels, pushier this time. "He raped you?"

Niels didn't want to have to answer that question, ever. He regretted assuming it was what had happened to Viggo. He avoided Viggo's eyes and offered his hand to Laney. "Niels."

They shook hands; Laney seemed bored with the exchange, much more interested in Viggo than in Niels.

He turned back to Viggo, who watched him waitingly. Christ.

He ducked his head. "He tried. That's how I broke my nose; why I hired Griff."

"Oh," Viggo breathed, his body tense. He hugged Niels again, this time without the tears.

Yeah, *oh*. Now Viggo knew why the band stopped doing tours with *Quoth the Crow*. Now he knew Niels' secret Li had always kept to herself.

Viggo stepped away eventually, after a long hug that made Niels realize Viggo wasn't comforting Niels as much as himself, that something more had happened than Viggo admitted so far. He gestured toward Laney. "This is Laney. She's going to be my wife."

"Ja, I got that." It was only a little insane. "And this is her talking cat. Did you know cats domesticated themselves?"

When Niels said *cat*, the snow leopard growled low in her throat and narrowed her eye slits at him.

"It's a leopard," Viggo corrected, and the cat growled again at *it*. "Kyori isn't a cat. That's like calling her..." He glanced at Niels. "The bad word."

There was a bad word to call cats, besides *cat* and *it*?

"It's like calling you an ape," Laney supplied before she blushed.

Viggo laughed, a note of affection toward Laney there.

Where had this girl come from, if she was even real? How could Viggo think he was betrothed?

"Can I have more travel packs?" Viggo asked her. "Please? I'll come back."

"You're supposed to come to school here and learn about here." Even as she said it, Laney passed him more of those little tea bags.

"I can't." Viggo glanced at Niels. "I have a job."

Hey, far be it from Niels to keep Viggo from his betrothal duties to the girl with the talking cat.

This. Was. Insane. Niels pinched the bridge of his nose and tried to focus. Maybe a hallucination, maybe real. Viggo had been *somewhere* for two days and gotten from the studio to his bedroom without anyone noticing.

"You have a *job*?" Laney complained. Niels bet she didn't believe Viggo; how could a kid his age possibly have a real job?

"Ja," Niels told her. "And we lost a lot of money because you stole him."

Two canceled concerts, all those refunded tickets. Some people had taken them up on a fallback date in January, but a lot had wanted refunds because shit like school and college got in the way of January concerts.

"Saved him," Laney huffed. "Minor difference there."

She clapped her hands, and the mess of pencils, plant herbs, and papers on her vanity all organized and cleaned themselves.

Magic.

No amount of nose-bridge-pinching would make this go away. Niels gave up and dropped his hand.

"Laney," Viggo said, and he sounded like a kid version of Far trying to convince Mor to let Niels fry klejner all those years ago. "Please. I want to be here. This place is so cool." He took her hand and tugged her toward the bed and Kyori. "And amazing. But I have to..." He looked at Laney. "Come with me. Move in with me."

"I'm an *heir*," Laney said. "I can't just leave, they'd find me!"

"You're in hiding, right? So hide in my realm." Viggo's expression was so earnest, so hopeful, so...disgusting pure love. That must have been how Niels looked at Li when he was little, before she said no.

How could Viggo love someone he'd just met? Niels had known Li for months before he realized how he felt about her.

Laney bit her lip, equally infatuated. Niels could *feel* how much she wanted this to work, despite her words. "Your realm isn't warded. We'll just have to visit each other."

"I'll ward it," Viggo insisted.

They had a staring contest, all chemistry and stubbornness.

Kyori stretched languidly on the bed. "This has been the last 48 hours of my life."

Viggo growled at her. "We're negotiating."

Clearly.

At this rate, she would be pregnant by dinner time, except they were both *so* young.

Niels changed the subject, away from 'negotiations' and onto something that wouldn't result in tween pregnancy. "Why doesn't anyone know about this shit?"

Viggo shrugged. "Magic is illegal in our world. I..." He sighed.

"Let's go home." He grabbed some extra travel packs from a jar on Laney's vanity. "And visit."

"No! Stay?" Laney pleaded. "One more night?"

Viggo looked at Niels, full of desperate hope.

"What the hell will we tell the police?" Niels asked him. They couldn't just go back to his apartment — which *he* was now missing from — and tell the cops *Oh yeah, we went to this alternate place where Viggo's betrothed, and the not-cats talk.*

Viggo stared at his hands. "What about...what if we get a boat, and we put me out to sea, and say I wanted to go to Denmark without the paparazzi knowing?"

The media and the police might buy that story, but Mor would be a different challenge. Still...it could work. Viggo was stubborn enough to keep it from Mor. "And how do I tell people where in the Atlantic to find you?"

"We get a fisherman to pick me up at sea," Viggo said, like that part would be easy. "We can transport me to sea, right? In a canoe?"

"Easy."

Viggo grinned at Niels. "See? It will be fine. And if you caught anything from Dylan, these people can cure you. They can cure anything."

Niels shook his head. "I said Dylan *almost* got me."

Viggo lay back against Laney's bed, using the leopard as a pillow. Niels wasn't sure that was a wise move. He liked how safe he was way over here by the bedroom door.

Viggo, though...he wanted to stay. Maybe more even than he wanted the band. "What if we did shows here?"

Viggo sat upright, earning another growl from Kyori. "Yes!" He crossed over to Laney's vanity and rifled through a bowl of different little pouches like the tea bags but different colors. He whispered something to Laney, who helped him find one, and a second later one of the band's CDs appeared in his hand. He held it up for Laney to see.

"You have magic?" Niels asked, because it seemed more like Viggo had known what he was doing than like Laney guided him.

Laney smiled at Viggo. "We're betrothed."

That explained nothing about Viggo being able to do magic. Niels should have realized this ages ago, when Viggo brought them here, but he'd been too distracted by the fact of *being here* to realize that Viggo had changed.

"I was raped too," Viggo joked, this time without cringing. "In my soul."

Laney turned away from him. "Next time I won't save you."

Viggo caught her arm and spun her gently back toward him. "Thank you for finding me. I didn't mean it...I don't see you that way. You found me."

She rested her palm flat against Viggo's chest. "I'd do it again, even if it made you mad again."

Well if that wasn't a profession of love, Niels didn't know what was. Even Niels hadn't gotten that much from Li, just a promise of *if* then *maybe*.

Niels realized he was feeling envy; no one had ever looked at him like that, touched him like that, except for Li the one time. Viggo had something so real it was practically tangible, and he reciprocated it fiercely.

Niels had *that one kiss a few years ago* and a girl he would love forever even if she never looked at him the way Laney looked at Viggo. It sucked.

Viggo looked at Niels, oblivious to his envy. "Want to get lunch, or is Mor about to explode?"

Explode? No, Mor was flat and defeated, not explosive.

"Viggo, everyone thinks you're dead."

It came out as a whisper, but Viggo missed the gravity of the situation. "So? I can be dead a little longer."

"Ja?" Niels challenged.

Viggo stretched across the bed and raised the blinds. Through the window, Niels saw a sprawling upper class neighborhood that could easily have fit in at home, especially in Connecticut or Upstate New York. "A whole world of people and things you've never seen. We *have* to come back."

Ja, they did. "We will. But we have to help Mor first." She couldn't afford this level of stress now that Viggo was fine. She needed to know, to feel better before her health declined because of this. "Maybe after..."

His heart skipped in his chest. Holy shit. He focused on Viggo, intense. "You said they could heal me if I caught anything?"

Viggo nodded.

"What if we can save Mor?" Niels asked.

Viggo's eyebrows shot up. "That was my plan." He was so full of shit. He turned to Laney. "Our mor is dying. She has a disease in her blood. Can you give her something to treat her, so she heals?"

Niels waited, breath held, and watched Laney think her way through that question. In a soft voice, she said. "Not today. And I'm not just saying that to make sure you come back. The healing stuff is hard to get."

"When?" Viggo asked.

She bit her lip again, more distressed this time. "I'll figure it out. As soon as I get some, I'll give it to you. I promise. I *promise*." She quick-kissed him on the lips and turned an interesting shade of purple.

"See?" Viggo said to Niels. He blushed too. "Betrothed isn't bad, because I like girls."

He was talking about Far and Mor's betrothal when they were about Viggo's age. Maybe Far's whole life would have been different if he'd been allowed to be gay.

Then again, Niels and Viggo and their sister Cille wouldn't exist

"Fine," Niels said. He could see the affection there, but he couldn't understand how someone as young as Viggo could feel that in so little time knowing someone. "But right now we have to go." He nodded to Laney. "It was nice to meet you."

She was his future sister-in-law, if Viggo took the betrothal thing seriously. He wondered what that made the not-cat...a pet? Another sister-in-law?

"Meeting me was torture, though," Kyori teased.

Viggo pounced her and for a second they wrestled on the bed.

Kyori pinned Viggo against the bed, a predatory feline grin on her face.

"I'll be back for round two," Viggo promised as he scooted out from under her. He kissed Laney's cheek.

"Come on," she told him. "I'll take you somewhere you can be found." She pressed a tea bag into Niels' hand. "And you can just go home and wait for it."

Niels couldn't get over how easily the cat had flipped Viggo over on the bed. "You won't kill him, right?"

"She's my wife!" Viggo said, too trusting.

At the same time, Laney laughed. "I said energy was *hard* to get. I'm not wasting it on un-killing him."

Because *that* was reassuring. It didn't mean he was safe, it meant she wouldn't heal him if he died.

Viggo had a dumbass grin on his face. He wouldn't go anywhere without Laney, that much was obvious.

Niels sighed and hugged him. He held up the tea bag. "How do I use this thing?"

Laney gestured with her hand: "Hold it out like this, and imagine wherever you want to go. When you drop it, you'll go there."

"Do I have magic?" How *could* he have magic and not know?

Laney laughed. "No, I did the magic part. That's like...eating supper and asking if you're a cook."

"Got it," Niels said. He looked at Viggo one last time. This better fucking work, or he'd be...no wait. How could he come back? He grabbed a few more of the tea bags in case Viggo never came home.

Satisfied, he dropped one of the bags and imagined his bedroom.

He was there in an instant.

Magic was *real*. Viggo better come home.

He wet his hair so he could say he'd been in the shower, and he rejoined everyone in the living room. No one seemed to care that he'd been gone. Li sat close to him on the floor near the enormous window.

Niels looked out at the ocean. Viggo better be out there in a canoe *with* a life vest.

Li rested her hand on Niels' knee. "You okay?" she asked.

She probably sensed his weird tension, his hope, but he couldn't say a thing about it. He shook his head.

Here she was, so perfect and so out of reach. He wished there was something he could say — or do — to get her to look at him the way Laney looked at Viggo.

He wished there were words for that feeling, the forever-loss that came from knowing she didn't care about him beyond friendship.

All he could do was shake his head and close his eyes, close out the world, focus on Li's hand on his knee. Friendship was better than nothing; he had to accept the parts of herself she offered him.

They sat like that a long time, wrapped in a blanket of mutual silence. Finally, one of the cops' cell phones rang. She answered, quiet while someone on the other end spoke, and then she met Niels' eyes across the living room.

"They've found him," she said. "He was canoeing in the bay."

A spark of joy ignited in his chest.

Viggo was alive. He would come home and be safe.

And Mor...they had a chance to save her.

That was magic.

10

HUNGER

It was a Christmas of hunger.

Another amazing concert. Every crowd seemed to be bigger than the last, and this was at home in Manhattan. The energy of the band was intense, contagious.

Viggo only played about a third of their concerts with them now —he'd gone to school in France to appease Mor and only came out for cluster concerts and for the summer ones.

Only Niels and Li had stayed after the concert to help with breakdown. There had been...a thing, onstage. A glance between them, a touch, that made Niels' heart race in a way concert crowds never could.

Now alone in the back room, he couldn't help brushing against her one more time, testing that feeling.

He made it seem casual, reaching for his guitar. It was right near hers on the couch, so easy to end up barely touching, shoulder-to-shoulder.

She gave him one of her big bright smiles, like a gift. "That was amazing. I can't get over the crowds."

He couldn't either. The way they knew the songs, the way their enthusiasm worked with the band to make a better concert, the way they cheered after every single song.

"You were badass tonight," he said. She'd climbed onto the stage framework for her solo for one song. The crowd reception had been beyond anything they'd ever experienced.

"You liked that?"

Christ, he loved it. Way more than he should. "It was awesome. They loved it."

She nodded. "We should celebrate. I made you..." She took out a brown paper bag and passed it to him.

He smelled them before he touched them: klejner. "Christ," he breathed. He offered her one, like people fed each other cake at their weddings, and fed himself one at the same time. The powdered sugar, the sweet dough, the slight hint of lemon.

He closed his eyes and reveled in it.

When he opened them, Li's eyes were on his face, a satisfied smile. "I know you missed them last year. And the year before. If you want to come by...I have my place decorated."

He tried not to read into it. The last time he'd gotten hopeful, she'd rejected him pretty hard. He kept his voice casual. "Do you mind riding with Griff?"

She shook her head and gave him a long, intense look he couldn't figure out. She plucked another klejner out of the bag and popped it into her mouth. "Come on. You can shower at my place."

How was he *not* supposed to read into that?

Did she have any idea what she did to him?

He tried to joke. "And change into one of your leather dresses?"

He cringed. It was supposed to be *not sexual*, not *sexual*. Why did he have to bring up leather and picture her in one of them?

He reminded himself that yes, he loved her body in a way he tried not to because she'd been clear about *no*, but he loved her more than the body she was in. He loved her laugh, her overgrown smile, the way she worked crowds, the way she'd spent most of the last year coaxing Viggo into relaxing again after the discovery of magic, the way she collapsed after a concert because she'd put every ounce of herself into the show.

He loved the way she looked at him, too.

"Maybe something lace?" she joked back. It took him a second to remember the leather; he stalled by batting his eyes at her and he popped another klejner in his mouth so he wouldn't have to talk.

She laughed. "I have Tigger pajamas," she offered, referencing the famous bouncing tiger from Winnie the Pooh. "You'd look hot in stripes."

He *rawr*ed like Tigger did. "Fine. But I'm not giving them back."

He could sleep in them every night, have a piece of her with him forever.

She grinned, suddenly all Danish and prim. "Consider them your Jul present." She slung her guitar across her back and eyed the door like she wanted to race him. "You ready to get out of here?"

He picked his up, fake-calm. He intended to totally kick her ass in the race to the car. "I got you something too. It's down in the car."

"Ja?" she asked, eyes on the door.

He bolted. Out the door, into the hall, down the cement stairs that wound around the outside walls of the stairwell, all the way to ground level.

She beat him. She *always* won these races, even when he gave himself a head start. To be fair, he had her gift tucked under one arm and didn't want to drop it.

She bumped into him right before she stopped. He bumped back and opened the door for her. She set her bass into the foot well and flopped back against the seat, out of breath. "Hej Griff."

"Hey, Li." Griff was already in the driver's seat, engine running so the car was cozy. When Niels slid into the car — leaned up against Li again — Griff met his eyes in the rearview mirror. "Where are we headed?"

Under her breath, Li made the Tigger *rawr* sound too. Her eyes were on Niels, expectant.

"Li's place," he said. Then, to test, he added, "Probably until tomorrow."

Li leaned back against the seat.

Okay, then. Staying the night at Li's. *Showering* at Li's.

His skin tingled in anticipation.

Li, relaxed against the seat and Niels' shoulder, asked Griff, "How are JD and Johnny?"

Griff's son and grandson were a single-dad plus sick kid combo, and the baby's health changed almost daily.

"He's..." Griff met Niels' eyes in the rearview before he dodged the question. "He'll be okay. Thanks for asking."

"Good," Li said. "We all put together a Jul package for them."

It was full of little things to keep baby Johnny entertained in the hospital, plus grocery store gift cards, a blank check to the hospital, and toiletries, books, and puzzles for JD.

It was Li's idea, not Niels', and Jace and Viggo had taken off with it, buying gimmicky things to hopefully make JD laugh when he needed to. Niels loved that it was Li's idea, that she cared about JD even though she'd only seen him a couple of times.

He brushed the back of his hand against her thigh, like it was casual, and left it there.

"Did you?" Griff asked. "That's..." His voice was pained. Niels and JD had a strained relationship because Griff often spent more time with Niels than with JD and JD didn't have a mom. "Thank you."

"They're at my place. I'll run them down before you go," Li offered.

Griff nodded as he eased the car to the curb in front of Li's building. "Do you want me to wait here?"

"Ja," Niels clambered out of the car and watched Li slide more gracefully across the seat before she joined him at the curb. "Just until Li brings stuff down."

He didn't want Griff waiting there all night when Niels didn't intend to leave; he wanted Griff home with JD and the Christmas present.

Niels had a surprise waiting for Griff when he got back to his apartment, too, even though Griff had insisted he didn't need anything except the privilege of driving Niels' Bentley Mulsanne.

Li tugged on Niels' arm, urging him toward her building. He waved goodnight to Griff and followed her into the lobby, into the elevator.

So many movies had people make out in elevators. Niels glanced at Li. She was still sweaty and flushed from the concert, with that post-performance glow all of them got. It was gorgeous on her.

He looked away before she could meet his eyes. Not that she would, but if she did...he didn't want to be staring at her.

When the doors opened and let them off on her floor, he trailed behind her, and followed her into her apartment. It was a tight apartment with floor-to-ceiling windows that looked toward the river. Along the left, a giant fish tank was built into the wall, and a baby grand piano ate up a whole corner of the living room.

He set his keys on the kitchen counter next to Li's. She passed him a stack of local delivery place pamphlets. "I'll be back, then I want my present. Order pizza? Or Chinese."

He doubted Chinese was open at this hour, but some of these pizza places were open 24/7. He called one, ordered a plain cheese, and went into her bathroom. No way was he passing up the chance to shower here. She might change her mind when she came back, so it was now or never.

Her shower had girl shampoo that promised to reduce frizz — he loved his frizz — and nourish his hair. He guessed the nourishment was okay, but he'd need to get the frizz back tomorrow.

"Niels?" Li called into the bathroom.

She was in the room with him!

"I'm here!"

He heard her move around the room, saw her blurred form as she moved through the room. "Your clothes are on the counter," she said.

"Your present's on the chair."

She didn't say anything, but a minute or two later the room was empty. He got out of the shower and dressed in the Tigger footie pajamas. He looked like an ass in them, especially with his blue hair, but he stepped out of the bathroom in padded orange Tigger feet and found her in the living room.

"Do you have any orange face paint?" he asked instead of saying hi.

She turned and looked at him, mostly silhouetted against the view of the city out her window. Her face was lit by the white bulbs of the miniature Christmas tree on her piano. The horse — a custom-made ceramic horse the artist had made based on several pictures of Li's horse she had back at home in Denmark — had been a long time in the making.

She only wore her underwear and bra, he realized. He should have said something more flirty than asking for face paint.

"No." She laughed. "I wish." She nodded toward the bathroom. "I'll be back. Is food on the way?"

"That's why I hurried in the shower," he joked, since he'd been in there at least twenty minutes. He held up his wallet. "I've got the tip."

What he wanted to do was cross the room and kiss her, but he didn't know if it was allowed. So he stood there with his wallet in the air like an offering, and watched her walk into the bathroom.

While she was gone, the pizza delivery arrived. Niels set the open box on the counter and sat at the piano. He could play music and see the bathroom door when she came out.

He played Christmas songs...Nissemand, of course, and then others...some English, some Danish. He was on *All I Want for Christmas Is You* when Li stepped out of the bathroom, fully naked, and dressed there in the doorway. She slid into satin shorts and a camisole, both the same shade of periwinkle.

Thank Christ for the piano. It distracted him, left him in peace to panic way across the room from her.

The last time he'd kissed her, touched her, let himself act on his feelings, she'd rejected him. Now she was so blunt about this. There was no more confusion, no more uncertainty about her intentions.

Tonight would be an amazing night. If he didn't mess it up. And then maybe all the future nights could be amazing too. Maybe they could move in together, go public as a couple...

She bit into a slice of pizza. "Mmm."

She sat on the couch, so he joined her there with a slice of pizza.

He liked the way their shoulders lined up, just about even. He liked the way her damp hair clung in curls against her neck and shoulders.

"What is Viggo doing tonight?" she asked. "Think he needs company?"

Viggo? Who gave a fuck what Viggo was up to? "He and his French boarding school friend are having a horror movie marathon."

Li set a box on his lap. He decided to keep it there all night, since the Tigger costume didn't leave much room for anatomical concealment.

"For you," Li said.

Oh, it was a present, not a lap concealer. "Besides the klejner?"

He opened the box and unfolded the tissue paper around the heavy wooden object inside. When he'd unwrapped it, he saw a carved wooden caravel, with skulls carved into the waves that broke against the boat's hull. On the deck of the boat was a small army of skeleton pirates, and in front of the wheel...miniature versions of the whole band.

"Holy shit," Niels breathed. "This is way cooler than a horse."

He looked up at her face, at her familiar blue eyes and her one crooked tooth.

"I made it," She said with a shrug. "I love the horse."

He kissed her, less quick than the first time they'd ever kissed.

She pushed him away.

Shit. He'd misread things again. He *never* wanted her to feel about him the way Dylan had made him feel. He leaned back, away from her. "Sorry. I-" He didn't know what to say.

She touched her finger to his lips, a huge smile on hers. "I had pizza in my mouth."

That made sense, and it wasn't a rejection. He nodded, and she caught him mid-nod, in a deep kiss that evolved into her pushing the box away and straddling him. She held his face at first, and then moved her hands down his body, feeling all of him; kissing all of him.

His hands wended their way down her shoulders, down her back. He grazed her waist with the backs of his knuckles before he slid his hands inside her satin top. Her skin was so warm and so smooth.

He slid his hand inside the waistband of her shorts.

"Niels," she gasped, urgent and hungry in the same way he was. She wiggled out of her shorts and pushed them to the side with her toes, her eyes on him as she pulled him down over her on the couch.

He didn't have condoms. He'd never even *bought* any before. "I..." he shifted subtly away. "I suck."

She sighed and shifted further away. "I know. We can't. The band is doing so well." She reached up and pulled a glob of tomato-y cheese out of her hair. She laughed.

It was no. Again. It was his fault for noticing the damned condoms. "I mean I don't have a condom. But that works too."

He wouldn't try a third time. He was so clearly friend-zoned that she felt comfortable *changing* in front of him, probably because she saw him as a brother and not as a real guy.

Her voice shook. "Niels. I love you."

His heart skipped in his chest.

She had more to say, he could feel the weight of the impending *but*. "More than the band. But." Yep, there it was. "This..." she met his eyes and felt him again. "I want this."

She loved him.

She had no idea how much she mattered to him. "I love you too. More than you know. More than should even be possible." He kissed her collarbone. "I can't even notice other girls."

"Same." She used her finger to lift his chin up so that they sat eye to eye. "I love you." She cuddled herself into the nest of his arms. "Our secret?"

Was that...was it a *yes*?

He wrapped his arm around her. Their secret.

She shifted again so she straddled him. "I take birth control pills." She moved her body over him. "But let's keep this between us."

There was nothing between them anymore. It was the most amazing deluge of sensations, and through it all he got to look at her face, see her reactions, watch all of her tension disintegrate in his arms.

He kissed her, reveling in the promise of a future full of Li and love. "Glædelig Jul, Lisanne," he breathed against the curve of her jaw.

She kissed him again, finally his to love. It was the best Christmas present ever. "Glædelig Jul, Niels."

11

LOSS

It was a Jul of loss.

He lay sprawled out on Li's bed. She never slept over at his place because Viggo was there, often with Laney and the cat. Viggo figured out a long time ago that it was easier to transport to his bedroom at Niels' apartment than to try to sneak Laney and a snow leopard around his boarding school.

So Niels hid at Li's — also with travel packs, so no one in the band saw him come and go.

Li stretched in bed. Her bare smooth skin slid against his and she leaned over his face to kiss him good morning. "Glædelig Jul."

He ran his hands over her skin, marveling. "One year."

One gorgeous perfect year. The band had gone platinum twice this year — once in early February, and once again with a single in late August. Between March and October, they'd toured most of the world.

"I got you a present," Li said. She jumped up from the bed. "Wait."

She ran into her living room totally nude. When she came back, she had a breakfast tray and a small package wrapped in lavender and silver paper.

"Breakfast?"

He grinned. She must have prepped this last night and had it in the fridge waiting. "Breakfast," he agreed.

He would show her his present for *her* later today: He'd been faced with the inevitable struggle of *what do you get someone who has everything* and he'd realized she'd been in the same shitty apartment for ages, even though the rest of them had upgraded to nicer ones right along the park.

Plus, with her in his building, it would be easier to come and go more casually together. They could probably get away with just living together and no one else in the band would even know.

He ate one of the pieces of cubed honeydew. "I got you a present too."

"Mine first." She passed him the little wrapped package.

He ate a cube of cheese and focused on separating the paper from the present without tearing it. Li's wrapping paper jobs were always works of art in themselves. "Another one?" he teased while he opened. She'd *just* gotten him an original Queen vinyl for his birthday.

She laughed and watched him unearth the small wooden guitar ornament. It was the same carving style as the boat she'd given him last year. This ornament was another of her carvings. He could see it fitting in with his small ornament collection, having a special place on his tree, but for now...

He looped the string over his ear and let the guitar dangle like an earring. "Yours will have to wait until after the soup kitchen," he warned.

They would spend their day serving the city's homeless with the rest of the band, incognito.

Li laughed and reached out to swing the ornament. "I made similar ones for the band so no one is suspicious. But we should tell them."

"About us? Viggo..." Viggo would be pissed. He'd been pretty fucking clear about them not dating.

"Ja." A huge smile swallowed the lower half of Li's face. "Because." She handed him another present, one she pulled out from under the bed. This was wrapped in a pale green paper with little balloons etched on it in a glossy cream color.

He opened this one just as carefully. Inside was a little tiny yellow outfit with a fuzzy teddy bear on the shirt.

It was tiny, like...like baby clothes. He looked up at her.

Her smile was more tentative now. "I'm fifteen weeks."

He hugged the outfit against his chest and then realized he should be hugging her instead. "Li!" *Now* he squeezed her into a massive hug that wasn't too massive, because...

Baby. They were going to have a baby.

Li kissed him, melted against him.

"Wait wait wait." He pushed her away, lowered her on the bed, and studied her belly, the little rise between her hips. There was a *baby* in there, a whole person who would exist because he and Li loved each other, because they wanted the baby.

He kissed her belly. "I should be making *you* surprise breakfasts. Are you on those baby vitamins?"

She nodded. "I just got them. I didn't know until last week."

Good. He would need to get baby books, baby supplies, a name book even though he already knew he would want to name the baby after his far, if it was a boy. If Li let him. If it was a girl...he didn't know.

"I love this," he marveled. "It's perfect."

She kissed him. "I love *you*." She grabbed a slice of toast and bit the corner off.

He wanted to marry her, as soon as possible. Engaged this year, married once the pregnancy was over and...he grabbed his phone and skimmed through the calendar. "June 24th?" he guessed. That was 25 weeks from today.

"The 24th.""

He sighed against her belly, completely content. More than content, he was happy. Happy and in love, and he told her so. Then he realized... "Holy shit! If this is a boy..."

By Danish law, Li couldn't inherit her family's title. She *could*, if she had a son before her far died, pass it on to the son.

She nodded. "But that's not why I want the baby. Besides...Falkhus."

Ja, having two estates was unreasonable. Maybe they could turn one of them into a shelter, or an orphanage or museum or something.

"Speaking of Falkhus...how hard do you think it will be to hide a living person from my mor?"

Li polished off her toast and tried to lift the tray to clear it, but Niels was a chivalrous asshole and insisted on clearing it himself.

"Maybe we tell your mor soon?" Li suggested. "We can book tickets tonight. First, soup kitchen?"

Oh Christ, she would be surrounded by homeless people. Most of them were harmless, but once in a while... "Christ. Be *careful* today."

She laughed, but he hoped she really would listen and be cautious.

They cleared breakfast and showered and dressed — slowly, interrupted a lot by touching and kissing — and made their way on foot to the soup kitchen. When they got in sight of the big double doors that led down into the basement Niels rented for the kitchen, they broke apart so no one saw them touching.

Outside the doors, an old woman with long dark gray hair and horrible teeth watched them. Her face was wrinkled beyond anything Niels had ever seen before, her clothes were dirty and ragged.

"Hello," Li greeted her warmly. She just had this open purity, even with the punk rock look, that made her especially good at working in the soup kitchen; she connected with people on a plane Niels never would.

"Hello," the woman said, heavily-accented. She said hello to Li, but her eyes were on Niels. "You want magic coin?" she offered. "One for each? Is pay for soup."

Li took it and tucked it into her pocket. "Thank you."

Niels hung back. "The soup is free," he insisted.

The woman touched his shoulder. Usually he didn't let people touch him, but he was so distracted by her gold teeth that he forgot to step away.

"All thing have price," she told him.

He took the damned coin and put it in his pocket. “Thanks,” he said.

He felt funny for a second. It was almost like being off balance, but...more like the *world* was off-balance.

He looked at Li, confused. He’d held her hand when they’d walked here. He could remember it. But where had they come here from? He’d met her somewhere. Not his apartment...

He blinked and tried to focus. Li. He’d come here with Li, holding her hand. She was important; she mattered. His brain was a fog.

It didn’t make sense; why would he have come here with her? He’d woken up at home. But he’d met her *somewhere*. Hadn’t he?

He wasn’t sure anymore.

“I need to...stop in the men’s room before we do this.”

She nodded. Her gaze was lost too, out of focus.

He stumbled away from her and the old woman, into the soup kitchen and the narrow hallway that led to the bathrooms. No one was back here except one other guy who stood leaned against the wall like he belonged there.

He was dressed in rugged clothes not often seen in this city; some kind of traveler.

Niels stumbled again and the guy caught him by the shoulder.

“Is okay,” the guy said in a soothing tone, with the same heavy accent the woman had used. “Soon you feel better, you no remember any of this.”

Niels’ body shuddered. He felt tears come from his eyes as a sense of loss overcame him. He felt like a little boy again, crying at Far’s funeral, except...no one had died. There was no reason for him to feel this way.

Why was he *hugging* a stranger?

He stepped away from the guy and wiped the tears off his face, ashamed of his baffling meltdown.

“When this all over,” the guy said. “In many years, you do this right, maybe you have your father back.”

How could the guy know Far was dead?

“Good luck,” the guy told him, and he walked away.

Niels went into the dingy yellow men's room and splashed water on his face to get rid of any evidence he'd been crying. He fixed his hair, smoothed his t-shirt which had an Isadora Duncan quote: *The dance is love, it is only love, it alone, and that is enough.*

Why the hell was he wearing this shirt?

Why did he *own* this shirt? The dance is love? That was bullshit.

He took it off, ripped the tag off the neck with his teeth, and put it on again, backwards and inside-out.

There: Now he wasn't dressed in a shirt he'd be ashamed to ever have a picture of him owning.

Love was a lie: Look what Far had done to Mor.

Satisfied with his outfit, Niels went out to the main room of the kitchen. It was less crowded than usual today, which he expected: There were *so* many extra soup kitchens on holidays, that people had more choices about where to go. They'd come back, when the people who only cared about the homeless for Thanksgiving and Christmas forget them again.

In the soup-and-rolls line, Li and Eddie stood together, ladling soup into plastic bowls.

"Hej," Niels greeted them both. He hadn't been sure they would come. "You made it on time."

The only one who wasn't here, was Jace. Niels stood next to Eddie. He tried to avoid touching Li too much ever since she'd rejected him.

"Soup is hot," Li said. She held up a ladle so he could see the steam rising off it.

For a second, something brushed against his mind. A memory? The sensation of Li's touch, of her looking at him like he was a treasure.

He shook it off; she'd set clear boundaries and he would respect them. "How's...life?"

Awkwardly. He would respect them awkwardly.

Someone new came in: An older guy dressed in jeans and a bomber jacket. Everyone else here was someone Niels recognized from other days, or was at least *with* someone Niels recognized from other days, but this guy was alone.

Niels crossed over to him. "Welcome, and Happy Holidays!"

The man looked him over with a grunt. "I used to be a pilot, once," he said.

"I'm Niels," Niels told him. "Here, have some soup."

He felt a pang in his gut, wishing he didn't have to do this alone. Li and Eddie and Jace all helped sometimes, but Niels was the one who talked to the homeless even though he had the social skills of a pissed-off llama.

"I'm Aalok," the old guy said as Niels passed him a bowl. "This place nice."

Niels shrugged. It wasn't nice, but that was kind of the point. If it was *too* nice, the wrong people would come. He wanted a place for society's outcasts to feel safe, and this place was just run-down enough to fit the bill.

"Thanks," he said.

He shoved his hands in his pockets, out of things to say.

There was something in the left pocket. He pulled it out: It was a weird old coin with huge bumps in it, mostly black with flecks of brassy metal that hadn't worn off yet.

It looked like a fake pirate doubloon from a costume shop.

He stepped away from the soup line and dropped the coin in the trash.

12

JOY

It was a Jul of joy.

Niels took a walk in the park first thing, because he figured it would be pretty dead, and he was right: Most families were home celebrating the holidays. He had his favorite seat, the Hans Christian Andersen sculpture bench, all to himself this morning.

He had a bagel in one hand, a green tea in the other, and a goose at his feet.

He was pretty sure the goose was rabid, unless geese couldn't get rabies. Maybe it was just an angry psycho goose that thought it deserved Niels' bagel.

"Look, just because I'm the only guy here-"

The goose interrupted him with a lunge at his bagel. He twisted away and the goose hissed at his shoulder.

"One piece," he told it. He couldn't feed homeless people and turn around and not feed a starving goose on Christmas.

He broke off a piece of the bagel and tossed it, far away.

The goose lunged again and got the rest of the bagel.

"Merry Christmas to you too, douchebag," Niels muttered. A jogger turned just long enough to frown at him and then kept running. She ran over the piece of bagel he'd thrown on the ground.

Niels was kind of glad he'd accidentally called her a douchebag.

Bagel gone, he scrumpled up the paper bag and tossed it in the trash. It took him about ten minutes to walk home, to ascend the elevator to his hall.

A woman stood in the hall outside his apartment, dressed in a champagne-colored wool coat and a hat so useless that hat pins must have been involved in its defiance of gravity.

"Mor," Niels breathed.

What the hell was she doing here?

"*There* you are! I've been waiting nearly half an hour. Where have you been, this early in the morning?"

"I went for a walk." He shoved his hands in his pockets and let her mull over the fact that maybe he had some healthy lifestyle habits despite all her disbelief.

She made a *tuh* sound and nodded toward the wall. "There's my luggage. You can put it in Viggo's old room."

Actually, he needed to find some excuse to put her in the guest room so she wouldn't see that Viggo still lived here part time.

He unlocked his apartment. "I've been...Viggo's rooms a mess 'cause I dump all my shit in there. So maybe you should sleep in the spare room.

She frowned. "Isn't that where you keep your instruments?"

Ja, he didn't have two spare rooms or anything.

He lugged her suitcase into the kitchen and plopped it on the floor. "I'm really glad you told me you were visiting, so I could clean and shit and, I don't know, *be home*."

She removed her gloves and set them on the counter. "I wanted to surprise you." She turned and faced him. "I know you felt like you had to do the band to ensure you could provide a stable childhood to Cille and Viggo if I became suddenly more sick."

Oh, shit. She didn't want to surprise him, she wanted to corner him.

"I'm..." He had no idea what to say.

She reached into her pocketbook and took out a stack of papers. "Tests," she said. She set each page on the counter individually, unfolded so he could read them. Each was a lab report: 24 of them, one a month for two years. They showed…

Impossibly, her antibodies had gone down.

Niels looked up at her face. He almost never looked at her and saw *her*, which was dumb because he'd never remember her if he never let himself see her. She had the same brown hair, same stupid hair twist, same warm eyes.

"What does this mean?" he asked.

She shrugged. "It means...somehow...I seem to be disease-free. It's a medical oddity. I've undergone a number of tests in addition to this, but no one can find any evidence I even had the virus, let alone what cured it.

Better. She wasn't sick, wasn't dying.

It was impossible. He wanted to believe it, but...*how*?

"This means," Mor continued, "that you can come home. Finish school. Stay in Denmark like you were meant to."

"You want me to come *home*?" Niels asked. He couldn't keep the incredulity out of his voice. She was legitimately insane.

She nodded. "If the reason you did the band no longer exists, then there is no reason to stay away."

"I did the band because I love music." He pulled out his phone and texted Jace: *My mom showed up out of the blue. Save me.*

He shut his phone off and pocketed it before Mor could ask to see it.

"You can play music at home."

"Not as lucratively as I can play music here."

Mor tapped the counter. Niels bet she was out of arguments, scrounging around the empty parts of her brain for anything that might work.

While she thought, someone knocked on the door.

It was Jace, dressed in a Santa beard. Li was next to him, even though they supposedly weren't dating.

"Hej," Niels said. He glowered at Mor. "See? I had plans."

Mor gaped at Jace before she returned her focus to Niels. "I came all this way to see you, and you're just going out?"

"If you had *warned* me you were coming..." Niels hedged.

Jace bowed his head to Mor, an apologetic posture. "We have a moral duty to serve the city. You're welcome to come, we usually hit the slums first."

Genius move. Mor wouldn't be caught dead in a sketchy neighborhood and Jace knew it.

But Jace was about to blow the soup kitchen secret.

"Moral duty to serve?" Mor repeated, skeptical.

If she found out about the soup kitchens, she'd get all weepy and warm and vindicated and Niels' whole persona in his family would be ruined forever.

"Caroling," he lied, before Jace could answer.

Jace smirked. "The most noble quest for knights of music." He cleared his throat. "And Li."

Li snaked her arm out and fake-punched Jace's shoulder.

It was a simple, friendly move, but it triggered a feeling, or the memory of a feeling. A joy.

These feelings drove him nuts. It was almost like he was living someone else's life, and once in a while the real him had memories that came through.

Except they weren't memories; they were wishful thinking. He could imagine being with Li, having kids with her someday, sharing Falkhus with her once the band retired.

He needed to let it go. He could see the painfully obvious chemistry between her and Jace.

"I would stand out too much," Mor declined. She dusted some invisible fluff off Niels' shirt. "Be sure to sing Nissemand."

He was such an ass; he hadn't even hugged her or congratulated her for being healthy. He hadn't really done much of anything except be a pissy jerk towards her.

"Be careful," Mor added.

Niels groaned, but Jace and Li promised Mor they would be safe. All of them — except Mor, thank Christ — took the elevator down to street level and escaped into the cold December morning. Niels had barely been inside half an hour.

"Do you want us to drug your mor so she passes out?" Jace offered as a jokey gauge of how close to losing it Niels already was.

He laughed instead of yelling, and hoped Jace took it as a good sign. "Please do that. How's your mor?"

Niels was such a jerk for being unexcited about Mor's health. Jace's mor was on round two of the same cancer, way less likely to go into remission. Having seen Far go through cancer, Niels had a bad guess that Jace would be an orphan soon, maybe even this coming year.

"Great!" Jace said, a little too cheerful. "I had her swing by and keep yours company. They think she might be in full remission by spring, the way her numbers are headed."

Niels fucking hoped so.

He couldn't tell Jace that Mor was getting better because first of all, Jace didn't know she was sick (unless Li had told him), and second of all, how could he tell someone with a probably-dying mor that his own sure-to-die mor was all better now?

Wait. Why did he think Li would tell Jace? Li didn't even know.

Niels shook off the confusion. "Let me just call Viggo and I'll catch up with you guys?"

"Ja," Li said. "We'll order food." They took their not-dating asses into Li's building and up to the apartment they'd probably woken up in together this morning.

Niels dialed Viggo's Frenchie cell phone. Overseas calls always had this microdelay that made talking a little painful. As soon as Viggo picked up, before he could say anything, Niels greeted, "Hey, douchebag."

"Hej," Viggo whispered. His voice was strained, somewhere between worry and panic. "We have a problem."

What, another one? Had Mor already realized Viggo was still doing concerts?

"We do?"

"Mor left Denmark," Viggo whispered. "Have you heard from her? Someone mentioned Guam."

Save the one trip to Calais, and the time Viggo was missing at

Christmas, Mor hadn't traveled anywhere since Far's death. It was some kind of weird self-denial ritual nobody but her gave a fuck about.

"Ja, she's here," Niels promised. "Very not Guam."

Viggo's relief was palpable, all the way across the Atlantic. "I flew into town. I'm...at the airport."

He was? Why was the phone so...pausey, if he was on the same continent?

"Shouldn't you be practicing declensions or something?" Niels teased. "Come here, you can rot with me. Visit with Mor. Wish you weren't."

Viggo laughed. "Rot how?" And suddenly he was there, right on Park Avenue. He shoved the phone in his pocket and grinned at Niels. "I was at the airport, when. Earlier. When I landed. Hej." Viggo hugged Niels. "Is Mor okay?"

"That's what's weird," Niels said. It was one of the weird things, anyway. Viggo's behavior was a whole other mess. Was in Denmark, no the airport, no the middle of Manhattan. "She's like...a medical mystery. Her antibody tests keep coming back negative."

"I've been trying new snacks from a witch website. Maybe one of them worked?"

Right, that made sense. "I've been mailing her crystals infused with positive vibes," he fired back sarcastically.

Viggo laughed. "Guess she didn't need them. Is...she mad?"

"So happy. Still clueless about all your concerts, though."

Viggo looked up, thinking. "I'll tell her I came home for Jul and she was gone and I was a flight behind her. Or I called home and left from school, so I was only...probably from school."

Or he could tell the truth, except he clearly needed to lie. The only reason Niels could think of for him to lie was... "You were already here! New girlfriend?"

Viggo cringed. "We can't tell Mor that!" His face had a soft blush.

"No shit. But..." Mor didn't know he was here yet. "You could stay at Jace's and *arrive* tomorrow."

"Good idea," Viggo said. "Do you think I'm too young for marriage?"

Who the hell *was* this girl?

"I think you have to be sixteen here. Minimum." He didn't know the actual laws because marriage and girlfriends weren't on his plate, so he just picked an arbitrary age that was older than Viggo. Sixteen was how old Mor was when she had Niels, and even though *Niels* had turned out like an amazing perfect awesome guy, Mor's life had been a mess.

He didn't want that for his brother.

Viggo sighed. "Girls hate waiting."

If *girl* hated waiting, then *girl* was immature and needed to wait even longer. "Who is she?"

"A girl I go to school with. I would have brought her, but her parents are assholes."

Niels thought he had come to New York to see his girlfriend, not...whatever mess Viggo alluded to. Niels still didn't have the truth from Viggo; he wondered if he ever would.

"It figures that you would find someone before I did," Niels muttered. *Years* younger.

"You should marry Li," Viggo teased.

Li was so...unattainable. Niels had made up his mind to let it go and he would, but hearing Viggo say it...Ja, he should marry Li. The trouble was that Li wanted Jace and had her little rules about where Niels belonged.

He made a resolution. He wasn't into the whole New Year's thing for himself: Usually when he found a problem he fixed it right then. He didn't need a new year to trigger things. Just this one time though, he resolved: By this time next year, he would have dated at least one girl who wasn't Li. For now...

"Mor is okay," Niels focused himself. Mor's health was what mattered. "Off all her meds."

Viggo hugged him. "She's going to live!"

Ja, she was.

Maybe it was a Jul gift from Far. Maybe it was magic.

THE END

BLUE NOTE

CHAPTER ONE

"Christ. Good*night*."

Niels must have said it a dozen times now.

His mom raised her eyebrows when he said *Christ* and shut the door in his face.

It was so nice having his mom visit — like an additional circle of hell designed for his suffering.

At least he had a guest room with a door. His bedroom had a door too. That made two gorgeous barriers between him and the bane of his existence.

But he didn't go into his bedroom. He didn't have a tv in there. For now, he went to the living room to unwind.

He sat on the couch and took his shoes off. He should watch a movie, relax before he tried to sleep. Otherwise he was just going to have nightmares of his mom all night, and that was the scariest thing he could think of.

Remote in hand, he leaned back and scrolled through movie genres — romance, drama, historical fiction romance, the Austen flicks.

Austen, yes. Then if his mom came out she couldn't complain. His mom was so into formal perfect, she'd even made him take fencing and dancing lessons when he was a kid. He'd stuck with the fencing, for the fun of it, and the dancing helped with his career, but he wouldn't have chosen either.

Austen would be perfect.

He had his thumb on the play button when someone knocked on the door.

It was just going to be that kind of night.

He shut everything off before he answered. The only people who ever came over were his band members, and the only one who came over without texting first was his obnoxious downstairs neighbor Hattie, who insisted she didn't need a phone.

He didn't need her High Holy Phonelessness commenting on the Austen thing. Having a conversation about romance movies — with the girl he refused to admit he liked — would be a nightmare.

She knocked again, more demanding. Christ. You'd think it was her apartment, not his.

He wrenched the door open. Hattie stood in the hall, her brown hair frizzy and wild, her face coated in a thin sheen of sweat even though it was December and fucking cold out.

How the hell was she so gorgeous?

She jumped at him and threw her arms around him in a bear hug.

"What?"

She never hugged. They had a strict no-touch rule between them to help them ignore the fact that they had feelings for each other. It was going well so far. Denial was a sweet thing.

"I was working at the soup kitchen and that kid that hangs out with Aalok was there, and..." She stepped away from him, enough that he could see she'd been crying. She straightened her shirt, pulling it down over the drawstring waistband of her pants. "Nothing. I just. Hey. What's up?"

What the actual fuck was that? Get him drunk on her scent and then back up and be platonic again? Act all freaked out and then insist everything was fine?

It was not fine.

He pulled her the rest of the way into his apartment. "Get in here."

"I am in here," she said, teasing despite the earlier panicked freak out hug. She turned and shut the door behind her. "I ran. I thought he might be following me or something, so I ran."

He side-stepped into his kitchen area and grabbed her a soda. He passed it to her. "Who did you think was chasing you? That Luca kid?"

Luca hung out with an old guy, Aalok, who claimed he'd been an airplane pilot. Aalok had been coming to the soup kitchen almost as long as Niels had been running it. He mostly kept to himself, but a few weeks ago Luca started joining him.

For a while, Niels worried that Luca might be a human trafficking victim or something, but Aalok and Luca insisted they were grandfather and grandson. They *did* look alike — same dark skin tone and puffy lips and sharp eyes.

Hattie nodded her head about Luca. "Yeah. Him." She sipped the soda. "He...did something weird."

Niels' back muscles tensed all at once. Hattie lived here, in Niels' building, because Niels had found her living on the streets after she ran away from home. She wasn't a typical runaway: She was running from her dad who had assaulted her a minimum of four times.

It might have been more. It probably was: The odds of getting pregnant *every* time you were raped were pretty low.

He scowled at Hattie, demanding answers.

"Not assault," she reassured him. "But..."

Maybe they had different definitions of *assault*. "Did he touch you?"

"My arm." She took a deep breath. "Niels. Do you think magic might be real?"

No. He straightened the framed poster on the wall — a blown-up image of an album cover — that Hattie had knocked out of place when she brushed against it.

"Magic like...Hogwarts and shit?"

"Maybe. But like. Other magic." She tucked her hair away from her face and pulled her denim jacket off. She was staying, apparently. He took her jacket from her and hung it on the extra hook by the door. "He touched my arm," she said, "and we were somewhere else. Then my mom was there." Tears welled in her eyes. "She's not dead."

Niels had no clue if that was a good thing or a bad thing. Were the tears bittersweet? Frustrated? Relieved? He knew which one he'd feel if he saw his dead dad again.

Hattie seeing her mom had to be a hallucination; the moving somewhere else...it was creepy.

"Did you drink anything at the kitchen?"

"I don't know." Her tone dropped as her voice calmed. "I don't think so. I don't know." She took another long drink.

"So you hallucinated." Niels' friend Jace had worked tonight too. Tomorrow morning, he would ask him if he'd seen any of this.

"Yeah, probably," she said. She leaned against him. Another violation of the respectful no-touch clause. "Can I sleep here?"

He stepped away from her. "What?" Christ, no. If his mom saw them together, she'd see right through his façade and he wasn't ready to discuss his feelings for Hattie. Especially not with her.

"I don't know." She shrugged. "What if he uses one of those things and comes here?"

One of what things?

"It's probably the drugs, but what if I had too many?" she said, with a touch of drama. She leaned against the wall, suddenly weaker. "I might OD. I just...please? I'll take the couch."

She wasn't acting high. He didn't have much one-on-one experience with high people, but enough to know she wasn't acting high.

Except for the crazy shit.

"What things?" he asked.

She looked off to the side, at the wall. "When he moved places, he had these little bags."

Didn't magic people have wands and shit? Not bags...

"Where did he take you?"

She shrugged again. "Just to the park. Then back to the kitchen."

He was sure it was a hallucination, but this was *Hattie*. Trying to get her life on track; she was honest and open. And Jace would've said something if anyone had touched Hattie's drink.

"And you saw your *mom*?" he said, because he was out of other things to ask and he felt like picking at that wound. Her mom abandoned her and her sister right around Hattie's thirteenth birthday and hadn't been heard from since.

Hattie hugged herself. He was an asshole for not comforting her. "Yeah. She's fine. She said she had to leave when I was little because it wasn't safe. Which, duh. But," her tone darkened, in a flippant way. "She didn't bring me."

She knew it wasn't safe, but she'd left Hattie behind to face her dad alone.

It wasn't exactly the kind of thing she would fantasize about her mom saying. A complex explanation about how her mom didn't have a choice, would be better.

Even *I love you and I missed you so much* would be better.

"Ja," he breathed. "You can stay here. I'll take the couch."

He wouldn't touch her at all. The last thing she needed, after what she'd been through, was his clumsy attempt at connecting with her.

"Excuse me, Mr. Poulsen?" she laughed, instantly more relaxed. Christ, she really was freaked out about Luca. He would have to talk to him.

She crossed into the living room, moved his guitar so it leaned against the coffee table, and flopped onto his sofa. "This couch is taken."

"You'll sleep better on the bed, and then you won't fall asleep cutting deli meat at work and chop your hand off, and then you won't lose your job."

She scoffed. "I do not sleep walk."

"No...in this scenario, you were *awake* cutting meat...and then you passed out and hurt your hand. Like when drivers fall asleep at the wheel, except you were at the deli slicer."

She sat upright. "I need to go to the hospital."

"What? Why?"

"One of us is sick. I'm not cutting my hands off slicing deli meat, Niels Poulsen. If your couch is worthy of your godly ass, I think it can take care of mine just fine."

He glowered at her.

She preened back.

"Fuck you too," he muttered. "Fine. I'll sleep like a god and you can sleep like a plaid couch."

"Mmmm." She stretched languidly down the length of the sofa, accentuating all her delicious curves and angles he tried so hard not to notice. "I'll feel so reticulated and fresh."

"Maybe you'll get a promotion."

She laughed and shifted to one side of the couch, leaving room for him. He stared at the seat. He could join her.

If he did, they might accidentally touch.

He stared.

She waited.

His mom was just down the hall, like some kind of self-appointed chaperone of his Christmas.

"Thank you for letting me stay," Hattie murmured softly. She pressed the red button on the remote and the TV came to life.

Thank God he'd turned off the Austen shit. "Want to watch something?" she offered.

He sat. Way over on the other side of the couch. "My mom's here, so try not to look like you slept over in the morning."

That earned another laugh that made him feel unexpectedly warm.

"Where is she?"

"My guest room."

Hattie peered towards the hall and then focused on the television, scrolling through genres, and settled eventually on the original *Night of the Living Dead*.

"Is that why you wanted to hide me in your bed?" she teased, as the car on screen eased its way up the hill into a black-and-white cemetery.

It didn't matter where Hattie was. "Either way, she's going to freak. So...will you be okay? I can talk to Luca."

He was going to fucking talk to Luca. He'd banned people from the soup kitchen before. He hated doing it, but if Luca was upsetting Hattie...

"Yeah," she shrugged, yet again. "I'll be fine. I just got spooked."

"Well your choice of movie should help."

She laughed, and then did the unthinkable: She slid her legs onto the couch, across his lap.

He kept his eyes on the television, his hands behind his head.

"I have you, right?" she teased. "God of Rock. You'll protect me."

She was never going to let the god thing go. That was twice in one conversation, all because of a joke on his business card.

He grinned at her. When he joked, it was easier to hide his feelings. "I'll stun them with my hair," he said. He flipped it for emphasis and for a second he could see the bright blue flop of bangs at the top of his head.

Without realizing, he placed his hand on her calf. Okay. He'd just rest it there.

"I've got you," he promised.

He bet they would fall asleep like that and his mom would have a field day the next morning.

That was tomorrow's problem. Tonight, he had a crazy girl and magic and zombies, and together they made tomorrow feel like a dream.

ELESARA BOOKS

Pieces of the Prism

A Very Fractured Jul

The Fractured Prism

Blue Note

The Last Salamander

Inheritance Key

Web Serials

https://warofthewicca.com

THE ELESARA SERIES

Thank you for supporting our project.

For more books, web serials, and updates:
www.theelesaraseries.com

ABOUT THE AUTHOR

HOLLY GRAF

Holly has always found a home in words. She began cowriting in elementary school, but moved away from passion in pursuit of something she thought she was supposed to be. From engineering to philosophy, law to chemistry, she somehow ended up with a BS in Accounting (emphasis on the BS). It wasn't until her accounting capstone that she realized what she needed to do. She turned in her final project, a written play about her experiences as an accounting student, and began her career as an author and a mother that same year. She shares her love of stories with her two children and can be found creating worlds alongside them.

HOLLYGRAF.COM

ABOUT THE AUTHOR

KRISSY MAY

Krissy lives in a chaos factory, which is run by a merciless team of miniature humans and their pets. She enjoys music, foreign languages, noise-cancelling headphones, and the smell of fresh-mowed grass. She has a useless degree in Physics and part of another useless degree in Nursing, neither of which helped in the creation of this book. You can see her through her co-authored web serial War of the Wicca.

KrissyMay.com

Made in the USA
Middletown, DE
24 September 2021